When Heaven Fell

When Heaven Fell

CAROLYN MARSDEN

CANDLEWICK PRESS
CAMBRIDGE, MASSACHUSETTS

First edition 2007

Library of Congress Cataloging-in-Publication Data
Marsden, Carolyn.
When heaven fell / Carolyn Marsden.
p.   cm.
Summary: When her grandmother reveals that the daughter that she had
given up for adoption is coming from America to visit her Vietnamese family,
nine-year-old Binh is convinced that her newly discovered aunt
is wealthy and will take care of all the family's needs.
ISBN 978-0-7636-3175-8
[1. Aunts—Fiction. 2. Family life—Vietnam—Fiction. 3. Poverty—Fiction.
4. Wealth—Fiction. 5. Culture conflict—Fiction. 6. Vietnam—Fiction.]   I. Title.
PZ7.M35135Whe 2007
[Fic]—dc22   2006051712

2 4 6 8 10 9 7 5 3 1

Printed in the United States of America

This book was typeset in Granjon.

Candlewick Press
2067 Massachusetts Avenue
Cambridge, Massachusetts 02140

visit us at www.candlewick.com

For my beloved teacher,
the Venerable Thich Nhat Hanh,
without whom this story would not have been possible

Chapter One

$\qquad$ 🌼 Binh's fruit stand was sheltered by corrugated tin on three sides and by a large umbrella overhead. The canvas of the umbrella had rotted away long ago.

"Mr. Thang! Come for your soda!" Binh called.

Old Mr. Thang crossed the street.

"My pleasure, Granduncle," said Binh, handing over the can of Orange Crush.

Although Mr. Thang hadn't paid cash for the drink, later he would bring a load of charcoal to the house.

Trucks and motorcycles passed back and forth on the highway, four lanes of black asphalt. Gray exhaust colored the concrete buildings, the speeding vehicles, and even the face of Mrs. Tran across the highway, selling her flat baskets of bok choy and ginger.

Every vehicle honked—either a series of quick beeps or a steady blast.

Binh took off the cotton mask she wore for protection against the fumes. She wiped her forehead with it. The day had been long and hot.

Binh's cousin Cuc rode up on her old bicycle, wearing a dress with red flowers. Cuc was a year older than Binh and half a head taller. Her black hair was cut in a short bowl, while Binh's fell to her shoulders.

"Did I get bicycle grease on my dress, Binh?" Cuc lifted the fabric to examine the hem.

"I don't see any. Or maybe just a little spot right there . . ."

Cuc gave Binh the clothes she outgrew. Binh couldn't wait until the pretty red dress—now dirtied with a dab of oil—would be hers.

Cuc not only had the red dress and a bicycle, but often wore colorful bracelets from her mother's tourist shop. The shop made enough that Third Aunt, unlike Binh's mother, wasn't always complaining about money.

Just then, three boys and two girls came down the highway in their blue and white elementary-school uniforms—white shirts with round collars, dark blue pants for the boys, skirts for the girls. Each carried an armload of books.

The boys went on while the girls stopped by the stand.

Binh pulled her cone-shaped hat low over her face.

"How much are the fruit cups?" one girl asked.

"A thousand *dong,*" Binh answered, studying the ground.

As each girl handed over a bill and helped herself to the yellow fruit, Binh kept her hat pulled down.

Watching the girls catch up with the boys, Cuc said, "They think they're better than us!"

Binh jumped up and imitated the girls' walk— stiff-legged, nose in the air. Then she picked up a small pebble and tossed it after them.

Cuc laughed, the streamers on her handlebars jiggling. Yet in spite of the way they poked fun at the schoolchildren, whenever those children came close, both Binh and Cuc lowered their eyes.

Instead of going to school, Binh worked at the fruit stand and Cuc helped her mother in the tourist shop.

Binh had heard that at school one learned not only about America, but about other places as well. School sounded like a huge doorway to the world, a doorway though which Binh longed to walk.

But Binh didn't like to think about school since her family couldn't afford to send her. School was for the sons and daughters of families who had large businesses in town and for paid members of the Communist Party. School wasn't for her.

"Let me have that last cup of fruit," Cuc demanded.

Binh shook her head.

"Please. Look. It has flies on it. You can't sell that."

"I *will* sell it." Binh slapped at Cuc's reaching hand.

Across the highway, two high-school girls bicycled

past, the tunics and loose trousers of their white *ao dai* fluttering.

Cuc gazed after them. Neither she nor Binh mocked the older girls.

Binh turned to the box tied to Cuc's bicycle. "What's in that package?"

"Paper fans. The bus dropped them off this morning."

"Are they pretty?" Binh asked.

Cuc shrugged. "I haven't opened them yet. But Ma is eager to sell them. I'd better get going." She pedaled off, her bicycle entering the throng of motorcycles and small cars on the highway.

The sun rode low in the sky, and Binh still had one cup of fruit left.

Binh's father, Ba, and her older brother, Anh Hai, would come soon.

If she sold enough, Ba might reward her with a small bill.

"Mr. Nguyen!" she called to a man walking toward the stand. "Come for your pineapple."

Mr. Nguyen, who owned the hardware store, approached. "Is it nice and fresh?"

"I've just cut it," Binh lied. The pineapple had sat in the sun all day, flies feasting on the yellow juice.

"Good." He handed her the money, helped himself to a toothpick from the small jar, and strolled away, spearing a chunk of fruit.

It wasn't a bad thing to sell old fruit to Mr. Nguyen, Binh thought. He had enough money to go often to Ho Chi Minh City. He'd ride off on his motorcycle, and then a day or so later, a truck would come with rolls of wire or boxes of parts for his hardware store. If he wasted a little money at her cart, the loss wouldn't hurt Mr. Nguyen.

A Buddhist nun came by, with her shaved head and brown robe.

Binh pressed her palms together and gave a little bow. On Sunday, she would light incense at the temple to make up for cheating Mr. Nguyen.

Binh wiped the metal surface of the cart with a cloth. She put away the unsold bottles of soda. Finished, she scanned the highway for a sight of Ba and Anh Hai. The highway was lined with the red and yellow satin banners of the Communist government. Some banners had a yellow star, others a hammer and sickle.

She looked down the road toward the motorcycle repair shop where Ba and Anh Hai worked, but couldn't make out their motorcycle in the stream of others.

Then she looked up the road as far as the large kiln where the Mai family manufactured bricks, a black cloud hanging above the chimney. Someday, she hoped to see more of what lay beyond that kiln.

Once she'd traveled the highway on the back of a motorcycle with Anh Hai. He'd stepped hard on the pedal and they'd zoomed out of the village, until the spaces between the villages grew greater and neat rows of tea plants covered the hillsides.

She'd held on to Anh Hai's waist tight, filling her lungs with air from the huge blue sky and filling her head with memories of all she saw.

The sun slid toward the horizon. Binh felt tired and wished she could walk home. But if she did, someone might steal the cart.

Just as the vehicles turned on their lights, Ba and Anh Hai finally arrived. It wasn't Ba's motorcycle they rode, but one he'd borrowed from the repair shop.

"How was business?" Ba asked, idling the motor.

Anh Hai sat on the back, his fingers drumming the rhythm of his favorite new song.

"I sold six cups of pineapple and twelve sodas," Binh answered.

"Good. That'll buy some rice."

Binh was proud of the way she'd sold all of the fruit. She handed Ba the *dong* notes from her earnings.

"Thank you, *con cung*," he said, and shoved the bills deep into the pocket of his pants. Even though Binh had turned nine at Lunar New Year and tended her own cart, Ba still called her "my spoiled little girl."

As Ba revved the motorcycle engine, Binh climbed into the space in front of Anh Hai, holding Ba around the waist.

Anh Hai reached one hand behind him and took hold of the cart. Then they rode off down the road as traffic fumes billowed around them. Ba edged the motorcycle in and out of the traffic, the cart following after them like a duckling following its mother.

Chapter Two

*B*a drove the motorcycle to the yard, where Anh Hai dropped the cart. Then he eased the motorcycle into the house, exhaust still pluming from the tailpipe. A motorcycle was safe inside.

Mist rose from the river, which slipped along like a sleepy blue dragon. Misty wisps concealed the bamboo, then drifted aside to reveal the shapes of long stalks and sharp leaves.

Ghosts lived in the thin fog. Binh's grandmother, Ba Ngoai, told the story of how soldiers had shot their neighbors during the war. Ever since, the neighbors' ghosts had wandered in the mist. Binh hurried across the yard to the house.

As she drew closer, she noticed Ma and Ba Ngoai whispering together.

When they saw her, they stopped their conversation. Ba Ngoai, barely taller than the motorcycle handlebars, folded her hands in front of her.

"Dinner is ready, Daughter," Ma said.

Binh kicked off her sandals and went inside. She heard murmuring behind her as Ma and Ba Ngoai followed.

Ba and Anh Hai entered too, dressed in their greasy work clothes, but with the sleeves rolled up and their hands freshly washed. They sat down on the floor mat, a steaming pot of noodles smelling of salty fish sauce in front of them.

Binh waited until Ba Ngoai had taken her place on the high cushion, and until Ma had sat down, before sitting cross-legged herself.

Ba and Anh Hai helped themselves to the food first, then handed the ladle to Ma, who spooned out a bowl of soup for Binh.

Binh brought the fragrant, warm noodles close to her face. She drank deeply of the warm broth.

When Ma reached across and dropped a bit of pork into Binh's bowl, Binh ate it up quickly.

After they'd finished and set the bowls and spoons in a large woven basket, Binh poured green tea into tiny porcelain cups.

Ma passed a plate of sliced papaya.

Normally after dinner, Ba and Anh Hai would go outside to sit under the arch of pink and white bougainvillea, smoking and watching the traffic. But tonight they stayed seated, even though dinner was over. Anh Hai unfolded the blades of his pocketknife and wiped each clean with the hem of his shirt.

Binh noticed a gecko on the wall: frozen, its toes spread wide, its head cocked.

The dying cooking fire popped.

Instead of rising to tinker with the kitchen fire, making sure that it was safe yet would burn until morning, Ba Ngoai remained seated. She smoothed loose strands of her graying hair toward the bun at the back of her head.

Binh shifted her legs. She wiped her forehead with the back of her hand, the air warm from the lingering heat of the day and the evening cooking fire. What was everyone waiting for?

Suddenly, Ba Ngoai folded her hands in her lap, chaining them together, fingers locked. "I have important news. My daughter is coming to see me." She pulled herself up very tall.

Binh looked around the room. Daughter? Ma was right here. Whoever could Ba Ngoai be talking about? Was Ba Ngoai getting old and forgetful?

Ma stared into the basket of dirty dishes. Shimmers of feelings Binh couldn't name crossed Ma's face.

Ba let his black hair fall over his eyes.

Anh Hai folded up the knife blades, snapping them in one by one.

Binh realized that it was she Ba Ngoai was telling. Ba Ngoai had already shared this news with everyone else. "But Ba Ngoai"—Binh hesitated—"Ma is already here."

"Binh"—Ba Ngoai's voice dropped—"I have another daughter."

The room was silent.

"Another daughter?" Binh asked, sensing a good story. "Tell me about her, please, Ba Ngoai."

Ba Ngoai shifted on her cushion. "During the war, I was in love with an American soldier named William. He was very young, and so was I. We had a child together. I called her Thao." Ba Ngoai closed her eyes and seemed to shrink.

Binh had heard such stories. In the war against the North Vietnamese Communists—or as others would say, against the Americans—many South Vietnamese women had had children with American GIs. But *Ba Ngoai*? This *was* a story.

Ba Ngoai opened her eyes. "William was transferred to Saigon. Maybe he died—I don't know. I lost contact with him. But Thao stayed with me."

Like the gecko, no one in the room so much as blinked.

"Things were very hard after the Americans lost and the Communists took power," Ba Ngoai continued. "The country had been through decades of war. We had nothing to eat but grass and insects. The American government offered to take all children who had American blood. They offered adoption by good families. I gave Thao away."

Ba Ngoai's head dropped to her chest. A tear ran down her cheek. "If I hadn't sent my daughter, she might have died. News came that all babies who were part American would be killed by the Communists. The Communists hated the Americans. And Thao had such light hair. . . ."

Outside, the traffic flowed as though nothing important was happening inside the house.

Inside, Ba Ngoai talked of things Binh had never heard of. She leaned forward, not missing a word.

Ba Ngoai cleared her throat. "I've tried not to think too much about Thao. She was five years old when she left. Thirty years have passed. Now, somehow she has found me. She wants to visit me." Ba Ngoai looked up and smiled, her face wet with tears.

Binh had never seen Ba Ngoai cry. She leaned closer. "When is your daughter coming?"

"Next week. She is a teacher." Again, Ba Ngoai sat taller. "Her two-week holiday begins next week. That is when she will come."

"What great news, Ba Ngoai." Binh smiled up at the gecko. The outside world was coming to her. Things were changing. She imagined that even the solid land between the flowing highway and the flowing river had shifted.

She placed both palms flat on the floor.

For Binh, the best part of Lunar New Year in February was the letters that came from the American relatives. After the American War, when life had been hard under the new Communist government, relatives had escaped in fishing boats. Many had ended up in America.

Now they wrote letters home.

Binh always looked forward to hearing the news. Some news made sense: a wedding, a new baby, a death. Other news was strange: a job working with computers, a move to a different city, travel to countries outside America (but never to Vietnam).

From the movies Binh watched at Café Video, she knew that Americans lived in sparkling new houses that never needed fixing. Americans wore beautiful new clothes that never needed mending. And all Americans went to school and learned all they wanted.

Except when they were shooting each other. Some movies were full of gunfire and stabbings and men driving fast cars.

Which was the real America? Binh always studied the relatives' letters, looking for clues.

She loved the feel of the thin blue paper, the envelope and letter one piece. She always ran her fingertip over the tiny American-flag stamp.

Sometimes money dropped out of the envelopes: crisp green bills with faces of American men on them.

Ba Ngoai always let Binh hold the money before she put it in her wooden box.

Photos dropped out, too.

Each year, Binh examined the faces of these strangers. None wore a cone-shaped hat. Their clothes were never missing buttons, nor were they torn. The men and boys had on suits like Mr. Luong, the town mayor; the women and girls wore pale-colored, ironed dresses. These relatives didn't look like family. Nor did they look like anyone in the movies.

No family member who'd left had ever returned home.

Now one was on her way. Coming soon. Binh placed her hand over her heart, feeling the dull thump under her blouse.

After a while, Ma led Ba Ngoai to the corner of the room and unrolled Ba Ngoai's sleeping mat.

Ba Ngoai lay down, pillowed her head on an open hand, and closed her eyes.

Binh lifted the basket of dirty dishes, which clinked against each other as she carried them out of the house, across the yard, to the river to wash.

The mist hid the river under its damp veil, so Binh felt her way down the slope with her feet. Usually, she shivered at the thought of ghosts. But tonight she bubbled with such excitement that there was no room for fear. She squatted and set down the basket.

As she dipped the first cup in the water, she held on to it tightly so she wouldn't drop it. There was nothing steady in her tonight. She felt just as fluid as the water.

Ba Ngoai had talked of Di Hai, her auntie, her mother's older sister. Someone who could tell her many things about the world outside this little village.

"Di Hai," Binh whispered to the dark blue silk of the river, "please bring lots of stories when you come!"

Chapter Three

*W*ord spread quickly among the relatives. Soon, Ba Ngoai's remaining brother and three of her five sisters, Ba's three brothers and two sisters, and all of their families, including Binh's many cousins, gathered under the arch of bougainvillea and under the shade of the huge spreading tree.

The white dogs and ducks wandered in and out of the conversations.

Binh and Cuc sat on the low bench and listened. When Cuc wasn't looking, Binh touched the sleeve of Cuc's red dress.

Ba's elder brother, Second Uncle, who had a long, narrow beard, said, "Americans make more *dong* in an hour than we make in a whole year."

"You mean *dollars*," said Fourth Aunt from her perch on a small plastic stool. "Thao is sure to bring dollars."

"Maybe she'll bring money for all of us," said Third Aunt, Cuc's mother. "We'll eat meat every night now." The waistbands of her skirts always looked tight. Second Aunt had died in the war, but Third Aunt had never become Second Aunt.

"Stand up a minute," Binh said to Cuc. Cuc stood while Binh scooted the bench closer to the conversation. She wanted to hear more about money.

The dog underneath the bench came out on sleepy legs, yawned once, and lay back down.

"She may not be rich. Teachers don't make much," Ba Ngoai said quietly from the chair where she was shelling lima beans. "Not all Americans are rich."

"Oh, but they are." Third Aunt leaned over and squeezed Ba Ngoai's forearm. "Compared to us, they are."

Ma, her back against the tree trunk, said, "Maybe she's rich enough to pay our rent."

That would be nice, Binh thought.

But Cuc, keeping her voice low so that only Binh

could hear, scoffed, "Rent money! Visitors from America always bring gifts."

"Gifts would be nice. But I want to hear stories about America," said Binh. "And," she added, "maybe Di Hai will talk about the war."

"Anyone can talk about the war," Cuc said, gesturing toward the relatives. "I'm tired of the war. You don't have a bicycle. Maybe she'll bring you one."

Binh imagined herself on a bicycle, not rusty like Cuc's, but new and maybe yellow. On a bicycle, she could travel far from home.

The next day, Binh didn't tend the fruit cart and Anh Hai didn't go with Ba to repair the motorcycles. With a rich auntie coming, who needed to work?

Ma was making a *non la,* a cone-shaped hat of young palm leaves, while she chatted with the visitors. She took long strips of bamboo and placed them in the notches of her triangular wooden frame. Soon the bamboo strips outlined the shape of a cone. When Ma leaned forward to talk to Third Aunt and her fingers relaxed, the last strip came undone, but she didn't seem to notice.

Binh pulled the frame close to her. She'd watched Ma make the hats, and as she listened to the talk, she set the final strip in the groove. She began to lay the white palm leaves over the bamboo frame, her thoughts flitting wildly.

Maybe her rich *di* would bring her dresses like Cuc's. Or a radio to listen to the latest songs.

Binh stopped work. The palm leaves had to be stitched onto the rings, starting with the tiny circle at the top of the cone.

"I don't know how to sew this part," Binh whispered, touching Ma's elbow.

"Like this," said Ma, turning to her. She held Binh's hand and guided it until the first circle was sewn.

Binh started on the second, larger circle.

"A CD player would be nice. And some CDs to go with it," said Binh's older cousin, Bien. He was almost Anh Hai's age and tended his family's vegetable plot, raising vegetables to sell at the Saturday market.

"With all Chi Thao has, she wouldn't miss a little of her money," Ma said, glancing at Binh's work. "If she gave us just a little, we could buy rice and vegetables— maybe some fish—without counting every *dong*."

Binh's needle made a raspy sound as she plunged it into the straw. Ma expected so little from Di Hai. Surely she would offer more than simple food!

"Why not a television?" asked Third Aunt, lifting one finger and smiling.

On the fourth morning, Ma announced: "We will keep the yellow linoleum. That is not so old. But maybe Chi Thao can fix the roof and the broken window. . . ."

"And even buy curtains for the windows," said Fourth Aunt, who often worked behind the counter of the tourist shop.

"And maybe she will even get you a refrigerator," Third Aunt whispered.

A refrigerator? Binh's heart fluttered.

❧   ❧   ❧

Whispers about America grew.

"Why shouldn't Thao take someone?" said Third Uncle. He lived in the north and had come down by train to see Di. "She is rich enough. She can take whomever she wants."

At Third Uncle's words, Binh shifted, the blotchy shade of the tree traveling across her lap. A shiver ran up her spine. *America?* Might she actually *go* there? Seeing America in movies had always seemed miraculous enough.

"After all, she should take some of us," said Ba Ngoai's youngest sister, who was just a little older than Ma. "She had it easy. She didn't have to starve, at least not for too long. She didn't have it hard like those in the boats."

Binh looked at the small house with its shattered window covered by a square of cardboard, at the layer of palm fronds patching the bad roof. She fingered the material of her blue dress, faded by many washings in the river.

But what if she were caught up in one of those American shootings? So many people died. Binh shivered again.

That afternoon, Binh put her hands on her hips and announced to her little cousins, Phu and Vi, "My *di hai* is going to take my whole family to America."

Of course, Vi and Phu told Cuc.

"I want to go too," she demanded of Binh. "You can't go without me."

"When we get settled, you can join us," Binh reassured her.

"And we can go to the discos and dance all night," said Cuc.

"And see the Statue of Liberty."

"I hear she's smaller than she looks in movies." Cuc flipped her bangs out of her eyes. "Very disappointing. Let's go to Disneyland."

Binh said, "Shouldn't we get Di Thao some presents to welcome her?'

Third Aunt donated a hand-carved water buffalo.

Cuc brought over a piece of gold silk. "I sleep with this every night," she said. "Feel it, Binh. It's so soft."

Binh held the lovely rectangle against the sky. "Are you sure you want to give this to Di Thao?" she asked.

Cuc squinted as though the gold color blinded her. "I do. I want to give her something nice."

"I have nothing to give her," Binh complained.

"How about this?" Cuc pulled a bracelet from her arm. The thin ring of metal shone with all the colors of the rainbow.

Binh wrinkled her nose, but took the bracelet. At least it was *something*.

"I'll fix her motorcycle," Anh Hai joked.

Binh wrapped the gifts in newspaper and tied them with string.

After the relatives had left, Ba said to Ma, "You are all getting too greedy. We shouldn't expect so much. Just ask your sister for a little support for Ba Ngoai. A little to make her comfortable as she gets older."

Binh pretended to be busy stacking the basins on the shelf by the back door. She turned slightly and saw Ma lift her face even with Ba's.

"We are the ones who have taken care of my mother all these years," she said. "She deserves support, but don't we deserve something too?"

A mosquito buzzed close to Ba's ear.

"We don't have to live like mandarins," Ma continued. "But the landlord is still waiting for last month's rent. And have you looked at the holes in Hai's shoes, the condition of Binh's dress?"

Ba swatted at the mosquito.

Anh Hai was feeding the ducks, tossing scraps of vegetables from the flat basket balanced on his hip. "I don't think Di Hai should come. She's already upset things. Everyone wants something from her."

Binh stared into the heart of a bougainvillea flower. Tiny pistils rose from the papery interior. "You don't want anything, then?" she asked, touching a pistil with the tip of her finger.

Anh Hai stopped throwing the scraps. He reddened like the bougainvillea, and smiled at the ground. "Just a motorcycle . . ."

Chapter Four

On the fifth day, Ba Ngoai and Binh took the men's work clothes to the river to wash. They massaged the grainy soap over the stains and rubbed the fabric against the rocks until the grease melted into the water.

After they had stretched out the shirts and pants on the rocks to dry, Binh lay back in the sunshine, daydreaming of Di Thao's coming. Maybe Di would wear a fancy American dress, long to the floor, with tiny straps over her shoulders. Pink, or maybe pale yellow.

"Tell me about Di, Ba Ngoai," she called lazily to the rock where Ba Ngoai sat. "What's she like?"

Ba Ngoai didn't say anything.

Only the river gurgled and murmured between them.

Binh felt sleepy. Perhaps Ba Ngoai didn't remember much.

Then, just as Binh was drifting off, Ba Ngoai spoke, her soft words echoes of the river itself. "The purple flowers flew off the trees. They filled the sky like flocks of butterflies. It was a beautiful sight, but really the sky was purple because of the fires. The soldiers had set fire to our grass houses. The draft created by the heat tore the purple flowers off the trees."

Binh leaned up on her elbows. "Oh, Ba Ngoai . . ." She could see Ba Ngoai's purple sky so clearly. Whenever war stories were told, Binh drew closer and listened carefully. The more detailed the telling, the sharper the pictures appeared in her mind.

Ba Ngoai was gazing off into the trees. "We ran. I carried Thao in one basket of my *ganh hang*. In the other side, to balance it, I carried a sack of rice. I ran with the others through the rice fields, into the jungle, where we hid."

"Wasn't Di Thao heavy?"

"She was very heavy. And the rice was equally heavy. But I didn't care then. Saving her life was all that mattered."

Sitting on the edge of the large rock, Ba Ngoai kicked her feet up and down in the rushing water as though the memories were kicking inside her. "When it got dark, sparks flew from the burning village. They flew over the rice fields. They were beautiful like the purple flowers. They were like little orange stars floating close to the earth. But those orange stars meant our homes were gone. And in the morning, I saw an owl, the bird of death."

Binh laid her head in Ba Ngoai's lap, shuddering at Ba Ngoai's memories, yet intrigued by this world of the past, one more exciting than her own.

In the kitchen as Ba Ngoai handed Binh a bundle of green beans to wash and trim, she said, "I'm happy my daughter is coming back. I've missed her all these years."

"Tell me more about her, Ba Ngoai."

Binh sat down on the floor and plunged the beans into a red plastic basin of water.

"During the war, when they heard the airplanes coming, the B-52s, the children ran inside," Ba Ngoai said, stirring the cooking fire. "The planes sounded like giant insects, but then the bombs hit, tearing our world apart."

Binh concentrated on rubbing the beans against each other to clean them. She'd heard this story before. It made her heart ache, yet she wanted to hear more. "Ma wasn't alive yet, though, right? Wasn't she born after the war?" She lifted a handful of dripping beans to the cutting board.

"Yes. The war was over by then. After I sent Thao to America, I met another man. A South Vietnamese soldier named Hung. Just after your mother was born, he was killed by a land mine."

Binh had heard about this grandfather many times. She snapped the beans in half, the only noise the crisp sound of the breaking. "I hope Di Hai will tell me lots of stories."

"Thao won't remember much. She left Vietnam when she was very young," Ba Ngoai said.

"Does she speak Vietnamese? Will she be able to talk to us?" What if Di couldn't describe anything?

"I don't know, Binh. We'll see." Ba Ngoai added three more pieces of charcoal to the fire. "During the war, I spoke a little English. I can't talk to Thao in English now, though. I've forgotten all of it."

Ba Ngoai tossed the beans into the wok. When the drops of water met the oil, they produced a loud sizzle and the fire leaped higher.

"Thao was only one of many who escaped. Remember Fourth Uncle." Ba Ngoai stood to take a photo from the shelf. "When he was just ten years old, he and his family left in a boat. After many days at sea, many days of hunger, the people in that boat were rescued by a cargo ship. The captain handed your uncle a huge red apple. Although your uncle was hungry, he held the apple to the sky like a sweet sun before biting into the crunchy, sweet skin."

That story had been told in letters. As usual, Binh

held the photo gently by one corner. It was always hard to imagine this man wearing a white starched shirt, the line of his tie even and neat, as a little boy lost at sea.

"Guess what!" Cuc shouted, riding into the yard, her bicycle rattling. She skidded to a stop in front of Binh. "Ma gave me enough money to take you to Café Video!"

Binh ran her fingers through her hair and smiled.

"She gave me money to get ice cream. But I won't get ice cream. I'll pay for you instead."

Binh reached out and rang the bell on Cuc's bicycle. "Thanks."

"Get on," Cuc ordered.

Binh put her feet on the metal bars sticking out from the back wheel. She held on to Cuc's shoulders.

As Cuc rode by the doorway to the kitchen, Binh called out, "Ba Ngoai! I'm going to the movies!"

Instead of following the highway, Cuc took the river path almost hidden by the evening mist. At the thought of ghosts, Binh pressed her fingers into Cuc's shoulders. Bamboo slapped at their bare arms. When Cuc drove over a rock, Binh's feet bounced up.

After one more bend of the river, they arrived at Café Video, a thatched hut open to the water. Just as Ba brought the motorcycle into the house, Cuc wheeled her bicycle into the café.

A woman with hair wound into a tight black bun took Cuc's money and gestured toward the movie room.

A big screen covered one bamboo wall while movie posters papered the other two. Men and boys smoked at the round tables. Small children sat on the cement floor close to the screen.

Cuc led Binh to two chairs in the corner.

"What will you have to eat?" the woman asked.

"Nothing," Cuc said, waving her arm, her bracelets dangling.

"No tea?"

"No tea," said Cuc airily.

When the woman had gone, Cuc pulled out a package of spicy candies. "Here," she whispered.

The candies were tamarind with chewy centers of hot chili paste.

"I hope it won't be one of those movies with a lot of guns and killing," said Binh.

"This movie's called *Let's Party!*" said Cuc. "Absolutely no guns."

The American movie bloomed onto the screen with the Vietnamese subtitles flashing below.

Bethy, with long blond hair, and Tiffanie, with short yellow curls, sat by a swimming pool, wearing bikinis.

Binh leaned forward, studying the blue pool. Pools were like the river, but calm, with no rocks or currents. She crunched into the hot center of her candy.

On-screen, the girls were talking on cell phones. A woman—"That's a maid," whispered Cuc—brought them a tray of sandwiches. Bethy began to eat one, then tossed it aside and sighed.

Cuc slipped Binh another candy.

Tiffanie laughed, her white teeth glistening in the

sunshine. She covered the receiver of her phone and said, "It's Marco. He wants to party."

Bethy dove into the pool and swam underwater a little. When she surfaced, the camera showed a close-up of her face, the perfect blue eye shadow still painting her lids.

Behind Binh, the mist grew thicker. If she listened closely, she could hear the river chanting its own stories.

"What does that say?" Cuc asked Binh. She didn't read as well as Binh and often asked her to read subtitles.

"She doesn't know what to wear," Binh explained, waving away the cigarette smoke that drifted toward her.

The scene shifted. The girls stood in front of a closet as big as Ba's motorcycle repair shop. They shuffled through dresses, holding them up, throwing them down.

"The maid will pick those up," said Cuc.

A man in front of Cuc turned around. "Shhh!"

Finally, the blondes emerged from the house and Marco arrived in a black convertible with the top down. Both girls rushed toward the front seat.

Tiffanie won. She gave Bethy, climbing into the backseat, a huge smile.

Cuc giggled.

The black car drove past the beach, the girls' golden hair blowing. Music blasted from the radio, then trailed off into the wind behind them.

The ocean waves crashed—what a pale sound the river made in comparison! On the sand, people lay under huge, striped umbrellas. *Like the umbrella over the fruit cart,* Binh thought. *But different . . .*

Marco's car zoomed fast, passing all the other cars.

The little kids sitting in the front laughed, but Binh wondered if the movie was about to turn into another boring car chase. Maybe there'd be shooting after all. She'd grown thirsty from the candies and wished Cuc had money for tea.

The black car finally arrived at a house, screeching up to the front door. As the girls smoothed their hair, Binh reached toward her own.

The party house seemed to be a part of the beach.

Big windows and porches opened onto the sand. Music pounded from a stereo.

Binh squinted at the food spread on a long table. She'd left home without eating dinner.

After a while, Tiffanie went for a walk with Marco, the waves breaking white and clean around their feet. When they kissed, the children in the audience booed.

As the sun set behind the silhouettes of Tiffanie and Marco, the English words THE END—Binh could read that much—burst onto the screen.

The audience clapped. Someone cried out, "Play it again!"

"Didn't we already see that movie?" Binh asked Cuc as everyone stood, scraping the legs of the chairs against the cement floor.

"Not that one. One like it, but not that one."

Cuc wheeled her bicycle out.

"Do you think that's how it really is in America?" Binh asked as Cuc climbed on.

"Why not?"

As Binh took her place on the back of Cuc's rusty

bicycle, she thought of how, in just a few days, Di Hai would arrive from the land of parties. Would Auntie wear a bikini and constantly hold a cell phone to her ear? Would she really take Binh's whole family—plus Cuc, of course—to that wonderland?

Chapter Five

*T*he Buddhist temple, mustard yellow walls covered with vines, was down the highway, set back from the road.

Ba Ngoai attended the temple every Sunday, while the others went only on full moon. But Ba had suggested that all the relatives—except for Third Uncle, who was an atheist, and Third Aunt, who was a Catholic—should prepare for Thao's arrival.

Binh followed Anh Hai inside to a courtyard garden with chrysanthemums like balls of golden light, rows of water spinach and purple basil, an arbor heavy with long bitter melons hanging among the leaves, and a bird in a bamboo cage waiting to be freed.

Temple dogs and a rooster roamed the pathways,

while fierce snarling statues holding huge swords guarded the entrance to the temple. Inside, Binh glimpsed the copper-colored Buddha relaxing in his dark sanctuary.

At the bottom of the steps leading into the temple sat a table bearing a large pot of sand where people placed lit incense.

Binh plunged her stick into the jar with all the others. As the fragrant smoke enveloped her, she prayed that Di would arrive safely, would bring all that they'd dreamed of, and would speak Vietnamese.

The temple gong rang with a deep, vibrating hum. The brown-robed monks and nuns, sitting above on an open porch, began their chant to the bodhisattva of compassion, Avalokiteshvara.

Behind them, a mural depicted the beautiful bodhisattva wearing a golden headdress, her thousand arms open to all who needed her.

Binh found a small plastic stool under a tree in the courtyard and pulled it close to Cuc. Cuc's hair was held back with a headband Binh had never seen.

When everyone had settled, a monk sitting quietly with his legs folded began a story: "One day a rich man came to the Buddha and his followers, asking if they knew the whereabouts of his runaway cows. No one had seen the cows. When the man left, the Buddha turned to his followers and said, 'That man is burdened by the cows. It's good that we have no cows to keep track of, no cows to worry about.'"

People laughed.

"I'm not saying," the monk continued, "that it's better to be poor than to own things. All of you know the difficulties of poverty. I'm only saying that not having to look after one's possessions is a benefit of being poor. Please think about your cows. Some cows may be possessions. Others may be ideas you cling to. Think of releasing your cows."

Binh shifted on the uncomfortable stool.

Cuc bent to whisper in her ear: "Only a monk would talk like that. He's given up the world. We haven't."

Binh nodded, but couldn't dismiss the monk's

words so easily. Everyone's hearts were heavy with longing for new clothes, a television that played videos, curtains for the windows, and a motorcycle for Anh Hai. The monk had called these things cows. If they had all these things would they be more—or less— happy?

Binh herself was filled with a desire to hear stories. Was that desire a cow as well? Daily, the desire grew within her to go to America. Was that the biggest cow of all?

Chapter Six

*B*a strode into the yard, announcing, "I've borrowed a truck to bring Thao home from the airport."

A truck. Binh sat up taller. That meant she could go too! She looked to see a small pickup parked by the side of the highway—red with a large rusty wound on the hood.

"Arriving on a motorcycle wouldn't look good," Ba continued, sitting down on the bench. "A truck is much better."

Binh had never been to Ho Chi Minh City, and she'd dreamed of seeing that faraway place where the buildings touched the sky and the stairs moved by themselves.

She imagined sitting next to Di Thao during the long drive back from the city, stroking the fabric of her fancy dress, studying her painted nails. They could get an early start on Di's stories.

Ma was hanging wet laundry. "You do need a truck," she called from the near clothesline. "Chi Thao will have luggage. You can't carry suitcases on a motorcycle."

"And the gifts," reminded Third Aunt. "She will bring so many." Third Aunt seemed to have forgotten her tourist stand and spent all her days with Ma.

The gifts. Binh's heart quickened.

"Hai will go with me," Ba said.

Binh stood up. "May I go too?" she asked. "I'd like to welcome Di Thao to her homeland." When she saw Ba shake his head, she sat back down.

"There won't be room for you once we fill the bed of the truck with the gifts that Thao brings," said Ba.

Binh smoothed her blue skirt. She wished that just

this once, Ba would choose her over Anh Hai. Even though she wasn't a boy, she was surely strong enough to help carry Di's gifts. And she, more than Anh Hai, had always longed to see the big city.

Usually, Ma or Ba Ngoai bought food from women who displayed their wares along the highway. But for Di Hai's welcoming feast, they needed to go to the market.

Ba took them in the red truck—Ma and Ba Ngoai in the cab, Binh riding in the bed. It felt good to go fast past the familiar sights, the wind blowing her hair. When they came to the motorcycle repair shop, Ba honked. Binh waved to Anh Hai, who looked up in surprise.

Too soon they approached the market—a sea of blue tarps stretched between poles.

As Ba dropped them off, he slipped Binh some money, saying, "Get your auntie something special for me."

Stepping into the market, Binh paused at the bright

colors and smells, the sounds of people bargaining and chickens squawking. Where would they start?

There were piles of green guavas; pyramids of the waxy yellow fruit that, sliced, made perfect stars; baskets of brown eggs; dusky tamarind pods; gingerroot; huge piles of baguettes.

Binh picked up a shiny tangerine. When she squeezed it gently, fragrant oil shot from the pores in the skin.

"Get a few," Ma said.

"Just a few," said Ba Ngoai. "When Thao was little, she always liked mangosteen."

The woman behind the pile of purple fruits said, "Take one, Grandmother. Try it."

"Thao always watched me split it open," Ba Ngoai said to Binh, prying apart the tough purple skin. "She would laugh when I tucked a bite into her mouth." Ba Ngoai broke into the white sections. She held up a section, and Binh opened her mouth to take it.

"Let's get some for Di Hai," Binh said, crunching into the soft seed in the center.

"We'll take six," said Ma to the woman.

They bought fresh bean curd, rambutan with the long red hairs on the outside, stalks of lemongrass. Ma bargained fiercely over the soybean sprouts. They got whole grains of rice instead of broken grains. They also bought sweet potatoes and corn. "These are cheap enough to fill up the guests," Ma explained, filling the bags.

"Do we have money enough for this?" asked Ba Ngoai, staring down at a fish swimming in a pan of water. "Thao always enjoyed fish."

Ma looked into her purse, then shook her head. "Let the others bring the expensive things."

Binh remembered the money Ba had given her. "Is this enough?" she asked pulling out the bills.

"Just right," said Ma. "That fish, please." She gestured.

Their money all spent, they carried the bags to the side of the highway and waited.

Binh thought of the American parties she'd seen in movies. Americans feasted on hamburgers and cake with thick, sticky icing. Would Di Hai like this food? Would eating it help her remember Vietnam?

She saw Ba approaching in the red truck. It stalled once in the traffic and everyone honked loudly. Binh dug her fingernails into her palms until Ba got the engine started again. Creating a cloud of dust, he pulled the truck to a halt in front of Ba Ngoai, exhaust fumes spewing over the bags of food.

"Wake up. They're leaving," whispered Ma.

Binh sat up and rubbed her eyes. The air was golden from the oil lamp burning on the ancestral altar, sweet and smoky from the incense Ma had lit.

Then she remembered: *Di Thao*. Di would become a part of her life today. Di would arrive in time for the noontime feast.

It was still dark out. The roosters' crows hadn't yet scared off the ghosts clinging to the morning mist.

Binh got up, crossed the room, and went out the open doorway. She slipped her feet into a pair of rubber flip-flops.

In the front yard, Ba and Anh Hai were already in the small red truck, dressed in their good white shirts, their hair carefully parted.

An old moon still hung in the sky, yellow as bean curd. *Not a good moon for new beginnings,* Binh thought.

Through the truck window, Ma handed Anh Hai sticky rice packaged in banana leaves. "Come back safely."

Ba Ngoai stood in the doorway and watched, her hands folded.

Ba gunned the motor of the small red truck. He backed up into the black cloud that came from the tailpipe and swung the truck onto the highway.

Binh watched until the taillights disappeared.

As Ba Ngoai cooked the breakfast soup, broken rice boiled with vegetables, Binh took three bowls from the shelf. She spread out the grassy eating mat.

Outside, the roosters crowed and morning dawned, a lime green blush above the hills. The day prepared itself for Di's arrival.

After breakfast, Binh swept the yard with a stiff broom until the dirt was smooth. Instead of collecting the fallen bougainvillea flowers along with the dirt, she arranged them in a circle around the base of the tree.

Then she buffed the floor inside with a rag, crawling on all fours. She felt proud of the way the yellow linoleum shone. Even a rich relative would admire such a clean floor.

Ba Ngoai placed tangerines in a neat pyramid on the altar for the ancestors. "I'll pray for the safe return of the travelers," she said.

"Including Di Thao?"

"Of course. For the safe return of my daughter."

With a soft cloth, Binh polished the glass covering the photos of the men with long thin beards, the women with their hair tucked under velvet hats. The ancestral altar was crowded with the photographs of those who had died in the war: Ba Ngoai's three brothers and two sisters, Binh's great-grandparents. In spite of the prayers, none of *them* had returned safely.

Beside the tangerines, Binh arranged fresh bananas and round green guavas, then lit a stick of incense, silently thanking the ancestors for sending Di Thao.

When Ba Ngoai knelt and bowed low to the altar, Binh bowed beside her.

Finally, Binh shook out an extra sleeping mat, checking it for insects.

Chapter Seven

As the morning grew brighter, relatives arrived, walking or riding motorcycles and bicycles. Some dangled an extra chair off the back of a motorcycle. All carried containers of food. The men set up the big table under the tree, near the river. Some used large knives to hack open coconuts, releasing the sweet, clear juice inside.

Binh cut sprigs of bougainvillea and put them in white paper cups. The shade of the tree dappled the faded tablecloth.

The house overflowed with people and the smells of fish sauce, garlic, and ginger.

"If too many people come, we'll make the food salty so they won't eat much," said Ma, stirring a wok full of bok choy and sliced garlic.

"This food is a good investment," said Third Aunt, undoing a button at her waist.

Cuc and Binh watched Vuong, the man who delivered water, bringing load after load in his *ganh hang,* the two buckets on the end of a stick that he carried across his shoulders.

Vuong had had an American father with very dark skin. People let him bring the water and handed him small bills in exchange, but because he had mixed blood, they would never chat with him or invite him in for tea.

"Do you know who's coming today, Vuong?" Binh asked.

"I hear it's your auntie."

"Yes. She had an American father. Like you."

Vuong looked at the ground. He was called *bui doi*—less than dust—because of *his* American father.

When he'd gone, Binh said to Cuc, "Vuong is nice. Too bad he's *bui doi.*"

"Your auntie is also a half-breed," Cuc reminded her.

"But she'll be welcomed like the queen of the world—with a feast and a big crowd."

"That's because now she lives in America and she's rich."

"Not fair," said Binh, watching Vuong disappear with his empty buckets.

Little children chased the ducks, their pockets full of candies.

As Ba Ngoai emptied the wash basins after cleaning the vegetables, she knelt down and spoke soft words to the ancestors under the earth.

Watching, Binh wondered if Ba Ngoai was telling the ancestors that her long-lost child was coming home.

Finally, Ba Ngoai straightened up and carried the bowls to the shelf by the back door. She went inside.

When Ba Ngoai came back out, she was wearing her best dress, a pink silk *ao dai* she'd kept hidden during the war. It had red dragons embroidered along the hem of the tunic. "Here." She held up a handful of pink and white ribbons. "For my hair. I need to look nice for my daughter."

"You do the white," said Binh, grabbing all the ribbons.

"I want pink," Cuc said, reaching.

"Oh, fine." Yet Binh made Cuc wait a little while she pulled the pink ribbons loose from the white.

First Binh wound white, then Cuc leaned in with her pink, alternating, as they decorated Ba Ngoai's neat, gray bun.

Villagers, especially children, peered from the road or pressed against the fence. The ducks had hidden in an old box to escape the crowd. The dogs roamed between the guests.

"The sun is already hot, Binh. Put this on." Ma handed her a *non la*. "The feast will be ruined if Ba doesn't arrive soon."

Binh and Cuc meandered in and out of the men smoking and chatting, women carrying plates of food to the kitchen, teenagers whispering together.

"Where's the red truck?" Binh wondered aloud. "Did it break down? Did Ba get lost in the big city?"

Cuc said, "Maybe your auntie isn't coming, after all."

She and Binh headed for the highway, shouldering through the crowd. Exhaust made the sunshine a dirty yellow and Binh's skin felt gritty. Sweat trickled between her shoulder blades.

Finally, someone down the way cheered, and then more cheers rose into the hazy air.

Binh leaned out to peek. "Oh, here they come!" she said, taking Cuc's forearm. The red truck was chugging slowly in the middle of the uphill traffic.

"Look, there's three people inside. That's Ba driving, Anh Hai is by the window, and that person in the middle has to be Di Thao!"

People edged back as Ba drove into the yard. Some threw yellow flower petals at the truck.

Through the windshield, Binh saw that Di had short, dark brown hair cut like a boy's. She saw no sign of lace or sparkles on her clothes.

As Anh Hai opened his door, people again backed up. He slid out, then held the door for Di.

Binh stood on tiptoe to catch a glimpse.

When Di Thao climbed out of the truck, she seemed to unfold her body, rising taller and taller, until she looked down on even the men. Though she had to be older than Ma, she appeared younger.

"Look at her, with her short hair, her jeans and T-shirt," said Binh, nudging Cuc.

"She dresses like a teenager."

As Di raised her hand to take off her sunglasses, Binh saw her fingernails were as short and plain as her own.

"She doesn't look Vietnamese," said Binh.

"She's too big and her brown hair is too light," Cuc said.

"She doesn't look like any of us."

"Why is she dressed so *plain*?" Cuc asked.

"Maybe she's poor after all."

The crowd parted as Ma led Ba Ngoai forward, holding her at the elbow. At last, a pathway opened up with tiny Ba Ngoai at one end, elegant in her pink *ao dai,* and Di towering at the other in peasant's work clothes.

No one moved or even whispered.

Binh held her breath.

"Chi Thao, this is our mother," Ma announced to Di, each word solid like a round river stone.

"Ma?" asked Di, stepping forward, her long legs quickly closing the gap.

"Thao," Ba Ngoai answered softly, the ribbons in her hair catching the light, the embroidered dragons marching forward.

When they reached each other, Di leaned way down to look into Ba Ngoai's eyes. Then they embraced, Ba Ngoai barely coming to Di's shoulder.

Tears ran down Di's cheeks as she dropped the side of her face onto Ba Ngoai's head.

Ba Ngoai clung fiercely, her shoulders shaking.

Binh said to Cuc, "I've never seen Ba Ngoai act like that."

"No," whispered Cuc. "You can tell how much she's missed her daughter."

The two embraced for so long that Binh shifted from one foot to the other. Her small cousins began to chase each other.

When Ba Ngoai and Di drew apart, Di reached into her purse and pulled out a tiny camera. She took a photo of Ba Ngoai and then flipped over the camera to show something.

Ba Ngoai glanced and smiled. She reached up to tuck loose stands of hair behind her ears.

"It's a *digital* camera," whispered Binh. "On a little screen, like magic, you see the picture you just took."

Ba Ngoai stood aside while Di turned to Ma. She held out her arms and, to Binh's surprise, Ma opened her arms too. Ma never hugged anyone, not Ba or Anh Hai or even Ba Ngoai. She never hugged Binh.

"Binh!" Ma called as she released Di from the embrace. "Come meet your new auntie."

"Wait here. I'll be back," Binh said to Cuc.

"But . . ." said Cuc, grabbing onto Binh's waist.

"She wants to see *me*," Binh hissed.

People stood aside to let Binh pass, and Ma caught her hand, pulling her close.

Binh smiled a big, welcoming smile at Di.

"My daughter," Ma said, putting her hands on the back of Binh's neck, gently urging her forward.

Di looked at her with narrow brown eyes just like Binh's own. It was the only part of Di that looked Vietnamese. "My little niece," Di said.

Binh found herself enfolded in Di's arms, her face right up against Di's pink T-shirt, which smelled not of expensive perfume but of laundry soap.

Then Di loosened her hold, but still held Binh by the arms. "We'll be friends, won't we?" she said in Vietnamese.

Binh nodded. *Oh, yes. Yes.*

Others stepped forward to meet Di. Each wanted to shake her hand, to have Di repeat his or her name.

Di took many pictures, and people crowded close to see the screen of the camera, the small children pushing through the grown-ups. People began to whisper her American name: *Sharon. Sharon Hughes.*

Binh turned the unfamiliar syllables in her mouth.

She thought suddenly of Di Thao's gifts. In the

excitement of seeing her, she'd forgotten all about the wonders that Di had carried from America.

She made her way to the red truck. The bed was large enough to hold everything her family owned. Binh could hardly wait to see what Di had brought. In her hurry, she bumped into a man and half tripped over a rock.

When she got to the truck, she peered over the edge. She stared. The back was empty except for a small suitcase. There was nothing else in it. Nothing at all.

Others also glanced into the truck, sidling over and peeking in. Checking it out, trying not to look interested.

Cuc said, "Maybe she brought small precious things like diamonds or gold rings."

"Maybe," said Binh. She imagined herself in pretty, dangly earrings. "I wish she would open that suitcase."

Someone had shepherded Di to the table under the tree. Fourth Aunt was filling Di's glass with ice and something cool to drink.

"How old are you?" Binh overheard Third Aunt ask.

Di laughed and the ice in her glass tinkled. "In America, women don't reveal their ages."

"But we need to know," Third Aunt persisted.

"Okay, okay . . . thirty-five," Di said, pausing before the words *thirty-five,* as though unsure of how to say the numbers.

"She talks so slowly," said Cuc.

"Like a little kid," Binh said, picturing Di as a five-year-old leaving Vietnam.

Binh strained to hear Di's answers over the soft chatter of the relatives. She wondered why the last question, and its answer, made Di's face redden. This was the first question asked in any Vietnamese conversation. Without knowing people's ages, it was impossible to address them. One word was used for those one's own age, one for those the age of one's parents, and another for older people.

"And how many children do you have?" asked another.

"None." Di reddened even more.

Binh placed her hand on the trunk of the tree, supporting herself. Having many children was considered good luck. "She's blushing—embarrassed about not having children," she said to Cuc.

"Or maybe she's hot."

Stroking his long goatee, Second Uncle whispered, "With the wealth of America—she could have many children."

"Your husband must be sad. No sons," said Fourth Aunt.

"I have no husband," Di replied.

"No husband?" asked Third Aunt, shaking open a purple fan.

Di shook her head.

The crowd murmured: *Thirty-five years old and no husband, no children. What is the matter?*

"We've heard you are a teacher. What do you teach? Mathematics? Economics?"

"I teach art," Di answered.

"People go to school to learn art? Why?"

"The same reason as here—to bring beauty into the world and to help people express themselves."

In the movies, Binh had seen art—pictures in frames—hanging in American houses.

"But do people make money with such skills?" asked Third Aunt, fanning herself.

Di spread her hands wide. "Sometimes money isn't everything."

"Only someone rich would say that," Cuc whispered.

Binh had never been so close to a real teacher. She wondered if, like the teachers in the village, Di wore a beautiful, silky outfit when she taught. And then, remembering school, she dropped her gaze.

Third Aunt handed the purple fan to Di. "Cool yourself down, dear."

Di moved the fan slowly back and forth, as though to wave away the questions.

Chapter Eight

*F*or Binh, there was something even worse than Di having no husband and no children, or being a teacher of a useless subject. "There's nothing in the truck but her suitcase," she whispered to Anh Hai.

"I know. She didn't bring anything else. Ba and I kept standing by the place where the luggage comes out of the airplane. Finally, she asked us what we were waiting for. We were embarrassed."

"With only that little suitcase, there was plenty of room in the truck for me. I could have gone with you." Binh scuffed the dirt with the toe of her sandal.

Anh Hai was about to answer when Ba gestured to him. He pointed to the truck and moved his arm as though he was lifting something.

"She must want her things now," Anh Hai said.

Word spread through the crowd. The children pushed to get close to the table where Di Thao sat. Even the dogs stopped scrounging.

Anh Hai carried the suitcase to Di and laid it flat on the chair beside her.

Everyone hushed, listening to the sound of the zipper as Di opened the side pocket.

Binh inched closer.

Di took out a small cloth bag, reached inside and brought out something wrapped in thin paper. The object fit in the palm of her hand. She handed the package across the table to Ba Ngoai. "For you, Ma."

Binh had been right. Di had brought tiny, important gifts.

Ba Ngoai loosened the paper and held up a pink stone shaped like a heart.

Everyone stared.

Binh narrowed her eyes to see better.

As though trying to make out something written on the stone, Ba Ngoai leaned close.

Di laid her hand over Ba Ngoai's. "I'm sorry it's in English. It says *Love*."

"Thank you, *con*." Ba Ngoai pinched her eyebrows close together as she studied her gift.

Di handed another pink heart to Ma. "For you, Van. This one says *Imagination*."

Ma turned the stone over and over.

Binh smiled. How had Di Thao known that they'd all been imagining many things for the last week?

Then Di glanced around. "I am looking for my little niece."

Binh stepped forward.

"This one is for you." She took Binh's hand, uncurled the fingers, and placed a small blue heart in her open palm. "This word says *Wonder*."

Small light veins ran through the blue stone, slippery as water in Binh's hand.

As she looked down at the rock, her lower lip pushed forward. A stone wasn't something she'd been expecting or wanting.

Di reached into the suitcase again and brought out

two large items, wrapped not in newspaper, but in a cloud of green. "For my brother-in-law and for my nephew," she said, standing up, balancing one object in each hand.

Binh peeked sideways. Maybe Di Thao had brought good gifts only for the men.

Ba and Anh Hai stepped forward.

The relatives leaned in.

Ba slowly unwrapped his present, and Anh Hai tore the pretty green paper off his. They each held up identical pink dragons carved from the same pink stone as the hearts.

"Like what my mom sells in her shop," Binh heard Cuc say behind her.

"Because dragons are a symbol of Vietnam, I thought you'd like them," Di said. "They're bookends. For your books."

Ba examined his dragon, running a fingertip along the flat side.

Anh Hai just held his, his thin mustache quivering.

"You put one at one end of your books, the other at the other end," Di explained.

71

Books. Binh frowned. Her family had no books. They had no shelf to even put books on. What would they do with these dragons?

Certainly, there was no motorcycle for Anh Hai.

She could feel everyone waiting for more from Di's suitcase. But Di zipped up the pocket and began to drink from her glass.

Binh clutched her blue heart in a sweaty hand. Wasn't this gift, after all, better than nothing? Di had brought it all the way from America.

Around her, she heard murmurs. Very low. Very polite. Binh knew that later they would say that these gifts had no value. And no use.

Binh said to Ma, "Shall we give Di Thao *her* presents now?"

Ma nodded, and Binh got the three gifts from the shelf by the back door. After Di Hai's special paper, the newspaper wrapping looked shabby. As she walked back to Di, Binh forced herself to smile.

After she handed Di the small packages, Binh pressed her palms together and bowed.

Di smiled. "Thank you."

When Di opened the water buffalo, she held it up and said, "Oh, how handsome! My students will enjoy this," then set it on the table in front of her.

When she lifted the gold silk from its wrapping paper, she exclaimed over it—"Oh, what a color!"—and touched it to her cheek.

Binh was suddenly aware of Cuc beside her. Cuc had sacrificed her bit of silk, but Di had brought her nothing. Binh glanced at Cuc's red dress, the flowers a lighter shade than they once had been.

Finally, Di opened the packet with the bracelet inside. She slid it on her wrist, the rainbows flashing in the sunlight.

Everyone except Cuc laughed and clapped.

The women began to bring the feast to the table: appetizers of sweet lotus seeds and winter melon strips, lemongrass beef, chicken wings in spicy sauce, corn on the cob, sweet potatoes, tiny dishes of fish sauce and chilies.

"Help us, girls," Ma called.

Binh and Cuc carried stringy green vegetables with garlic, yam fritters, sticky rice cooked in sweet coconut milk, the fish that had swum in the pan, now cooked, its eyes glaring.

Instead of eating, people urged the food on Di, even after her plate was piled high. Di had to keep saying no, sometimes a little loudly. Binh noticed that she set the uncooked vegetables aside and didn't touch them.

"The *Viet-kieu* are so picky about what they eat and drink," Binh heard Fourth Aunt say.

An argument broke out between Third Uncle, a northerner and a Communist, and Third Aunt, who'd always lived in the south and hated Communists.

"I refuse to call that place Ho Chi Minh City. That's its Communist name," said Third Aunt. "For me, it will always be Saigon."

"That's treason. The city was named for Uncle Ho, who helped us win the war against the occupying French and the invading Americans."

"I don't want to pay any respect to this Uncle Ho of

yours. Look at what the country is now because of him—a big mess, everyone poor."

The early afternoon sun shone hot, and Binh felt clammy all over. She struggled with a small headache and ate only fruit. She fingered her hair and wondered if Cuc could help her cut it short like Di Hai's.

Cuc swung by herself in the hammock.

Fourth Aunt was picking at her food, and Third Uncle gazed off toward the river as though looking toward America, his cup of sweet coffee cooling. They all had more to digest than food.

Chapter Nine

When the feast had been eaten, Binh sat on the bench as the relatives drifted off, their motorcycles leaving behind a film of black smoke. She called to the ducks until they emerged from their box, quacking and searching the ground for food.

As soon as the yard was clear, Ba backed the red truck out onto the highway while Anh Hai watched the traffic, beckoning when it was clear and jumping into the passenger seat at the last minute.

Cuc waved from the bed of the truck.

Looping her arm through Di Thao's, Ba Ngoai led her into the house.

Binh scooted ahead of them, reaching the doorway first. "This is our home," she said, gesturing toward the big room.

Di's eyes darted around as though she expected to see more. Her gaze lingered on the motorcycle parked in the corner, a small pool of oil underneath.

"Here is the kitchen," Binh said, pointing toward the side room. The cooking fire flickered, lighting the walls black with wood smoke. A cat lay curled, sleeping near the fire.

Di squinted. "Is *that* where you cooked the delicious food?"

"Some of it," Ba Ngoai answered. "Our relatives brought many dishes."

Her eyebrows drawn together, Di studied the ancestral altar with its photographs of the ancestors, the pyramid of tangerines, the bananas and guavas, the wavering flames of the candles. Then she set down her suitcase. "Could you please show me where the bathroom is, Binh?"

Binh led Di outside and across the yard to the small

outbuilding. She swung the door open to reveal a porcelain toilet set into the floor. Ma was proud of it: a real toilet instead of a cement trough.

As proof of how special the toilet was, Di took a picture, brightening the room with the flash.

While Binh leaned close to see the tiny toilet in Di's camera, Di Thao stared at the real toilet. "I think I need a lesson on how to use that."

"You put your feet on either side, like this." Binh lifted her dress and demonstrated. "Then you squat down. Afterward, you dip the ladle in the bucket to wash the toilet."

"I don't remember using this before. When I lived here, we just had a hole in the ground."

"Many people have holes, Di. This is a modern toilet."

Di laughed. "In America, we have toilets you sit on like a chair."

"I've seen those in movies. I would love to see the toilets in America."

Di laughed.

Binh leaned close to whisper, "I would love to *use* the toilets in America."

Di laughed again. "There's more interesting things than toilets."

"I would love to see those other things too."

Di didn't respond, but looked around, saying, "How do I wash myself?"

Binh opened the door to a small closet. Inside were a barrel of water and a bucket. "Here's water to splash over you."

Di dipped her hand in the barrel. "It's *cold,* Binh."

"Yes." Of course it was cold.

Di shivered. "I guess I'll wait until morning for a shower." She looked at the toilet again.

"I'll be right outside," Binh said, shutting the door behind her.

When Di came out, she said, "And now, if it's okay, I'd like to go to bed. I feel like I've come to the edge of the world."

Binh laughed. Di was right. This *was* the edge of

the world, not the center. Binh always felt she lived outside the place where real life happened.

"I'm exhausted," Di said, passing a hand across her forehead.

"You look very beautiful anyway."

Di reached out and mussed Binh's hair. "You know how to say nice things to people, don't you?"

Binh smoothed her hair and led the way across the yard. After the talk about toilets, she and Di were on intimate terms. Things were going well.

When she pushed open the door, Ma and Ba Ngoai sat huddled together, whispering. They grew silent when Di entered the house.

Binh walked across the room. "You'll sleep right here between me and Ma." She touched the yellow linoleum floor with her toe.

Di glanced around as though afraid of ghosts.

"Don't worry—you'll be close to all of us," Binh reassured her, unrolling Di's sleeping mat.

Just then, Ba and Anh Hai came back from returning the truck. Instead of feeding the dogs or organizing the motorcycle repair tools, they sat down next to Ma and Ba Ngoai.

They were all waiting, Binh realized. Waiting for Di Thao to unpack her suitcase. Now that everyone else was gone, maybe Di would bring out the real gifts, the gifts for Binh and her close family alone to see.

Binh smiled, thinking again of dangly earrings, or maybe a ring with a pretty stone.

Di pulled her suitcase close. The top banged open against the yellow floor and Di lifted out a small reddish book. "I have something to show you," she announced, settling down on the sleeping mat.

Binh's heart danced up and down. What could it be?

Ba Ngoai sat close on Di's one side, Binh on the other. Anh Hai, Ba, and Ma crossed their legs and sat directly in front.

"These are photos." Di placed the book on one knee and tapped it with her fingertip.

Binh's heart danced faster. Photos were even better than stories.

Di slipped the photographs out of the plastic holders and passed them around.

"These are my American parents," Di explained.

Binh found herself staring into the eyes of a man and a woman with hair the color of Ma's cone-shaped hats.

Ba Ngoai held each photo for a long time—examining the woman standing alone in a gray dress, the man with his arm around Di's shoulders, the three of them posed together by a fountain. Ba Ngoai looked and looked.

As Ba Ngoai watched Di put away the faces of her American parents, she asked, "Are you happy, Daughter?"

Di looked surprised, but said, "Very happy, Ma."

"Really happy?" Ba Ngoai persisted.

"Really. And now, dear family, good night," Di said. She lay down, turned herself over twice, and slept.

After a breakfast of rice porridge flavored with green onions and small bits of pork, Di opened the photo album again.

Everyone moved close and the room grew hushed.

This time, Di opened to a photograph of a white building. Dark green bushes grew on either side of a long path to the door.

"This is my house in Kentucky," Di said.

Binh looked up to see if Di was joking. The building was huge!

"Your house is almost as large as the Buddhist temple," Ba said, his eyes wide.

Anh Hai leaned over, looking at the photo upside down, his forehead lined with furrows.

Di flipped through the pictures. "My sleeping room, the room for people who visit me, the room for living, the eating room, kitchen, and toilet."

The room for guests had a high bed. Binh imagined climbing into that bed. No ghost would reach her up there. She laid a fingertip on the glossy plastic, wishing she could touch the lacy fabric covering the bed.

"That toilet chair looks very easy, very nice," Binh said. "I would like to try it one day," she reminded Di.

"Who else lives there?" Ma asked, squinting, as though trying to see people in the rooms.

Di shrugged. "There's only me."

Binh knew what everyone had to be thinking— this house in America had plenty of space for her whole family. In fact, it could hold several Vietnamese families.

"Aren't you lonely?" Ba Ngoai asked. She sat so close to Di that loose strands of her hair brushed Di's cheek.

"I'm never lonely. I see lots of people at the school where I teach."

"But you have no children, no husband," said Ba.

"I like living alone."

Alone? Binh looked at Di to see if she was serious. If she liked living alone, what would she do with all of them?

"And here," Di said, turning to another page, "are my Vietnamese friends. The ones I learn Vietnamese from."

Three women posed in front of a bush of yellow flowers, wearing Western clothes.

"This one is a teacher at my school," Di said, tapping the face of the woman on the left. "I met the others through her. This one is an eye doctor. And this one has her own beauty salon. She does fingernails. But not mine." Di laughed and held out her hands, showing the plain nails.

Binh ran her thumb over her own short ones, glad suddenly that hers were just like Di's.

"These are pictures of my school," she said.

This place was even bigger than Di's house—two stories tall, made of yellow brick, as large as buildings Binh had seen in pictures of Ho Chi Minh City.

Binh looked closely. So this was how a school looked inside—rows of desks and chairs. Instead of the blue and white uniforms of Vietnam, the children were dressed in regular clothes. Didn't they have money for uniforms? And such plain clothes ... plain like Di Hai's.

A few of the children had black hair. Just a few had narrow, brown eyes. Most had round eyes. Some hair was light brown like Di Hai's. Other hair shone like the sun. One girl had hair the color of the orange cat that visited Binh's cart.

Binh had an urge to put her finger on one of the desks in the front row of the classroom. She would sit right there. The teacher would hang her work on the wall.

"Tell me about these girls," Binh said. "Tell me all about American girls. Do they all have cell phones?"

Di laughed. "Most do. Other than that, they're a lot like you, Binh. They like friends. And clothes. They have schoolwork to do. . . ."

Binh bit her lip. *Schoolwork.* How would she catch up with those American girls? She didn't even speak English. Instead of sitting in that front row, she'd be hiding in the back. She'd have no work for the teacher to hang.

As Binh looked away from the pictures of the school, Ba Ngoai, glancing at her, said, "It's time for us to visit the house of the ancestors."

Chapter Ten

*P*lans had been made to take Di Thao to the house of the ancestors the morning after her arrival. All the relatives wanted to accompany her on the trip down the highway and up the hill on the other side of the river. They were waiting under the arch of bougainvillea in the yard, beneath the spreading tree. The men stood with their hands clasped in front of them, and the women leaned close to chat, crossing their arms and tucking their hands into their sleeves.

Children chased each other wielding long juicy stems notched so they snapped like whips.

Cuc, in a yellow dress with white dots and the hem let down, asked Binh, "How is your auntie?"

Binh paused. How *was* Di Thao? "She's doing well," she replied.

"Did she give you anything more?"

"Not yet."

Cuc made a face. "Why isn't she more generous?"

Binh thought again of her silly blue rock. "She showed us photographs," she said.

"Pictures?" Cuc wrinkled her nose. "What can you do with a picture?"

Binh couldn't explain how each photo opened a window in her mind, windows she looked through to places she'd never dreamed existed.

But she also thought of how instead of placing the photos of her parents on the ancestral altar, Di had slipped them back into the plastic and put them away.

She thought of how Cuc had given Di Hai her bit of gold silk. All for nothing.

Binh found Di Hai standing beside the big table, gazing at the baskets of tiny bananas, translucent yellow star fruit, and the purple lilies that Ma and Ba

Ngoai had prepared early in the morning. "So beautiful," she murmured to Binh.

The relatives whispered among themselves, glancing at Di Thao from time to time.

"Why do they all keep staring at me?" Di asked.

"They think your dress is pretty," Binh answered, although the olive green dress hung plainly on Di's tall body. She didn't add that it wasn't only the dress they talked about behind Di's back, but also Di's lack of husband and children, and her job teaching a useless subject.

Cuc came to the table too. In fact, she pushed herself in between Binh and Di, taking Binh's place.

Binh noticed that Cuc's yellow dress was ironed, making Binh's dress look even plainer.

Usually, Binh loved being with Cuc. But today her presence felt different, as though Cuc were trying to steal something that was hers.

"Your mother wants you," Binh said to Cuc.

"Where is she?" Cuc stood on tiptoe, peering out over the sea of faces.

"Over there," Binh gestured vaguely. "She was waving and calling your name."

When Cuc had left, Binh seized Di's hand in preparation for the procession. "We'll start walking to the house of the ancestors soon," she told her. "Ba Ngoai," she called, "take Di Hai's other hand."

Ma, Ba, and Anh Hai followed, carrying the baskets of fruit and flowers.

Binh looked back to see villagers coming out of their shops and children running and bicycling alongside, trying to get a peek at Di Thao. Binh's heart flamed with pride.

And Cuc? Binh looked back until she glimpsed the yellow of Cuc's dress. She was with Third Aunt, a safe distance away.

Walking along the highway, accompanied by the relentless honking of traffic, they approached the school, protected from the road by high white walls.

Binh heard children's voices on the other side of the wall.

Her hands grew sweaty. "It's very hot today, isn't

it?" she said to Di as they passed the school gate. Di mustn't look into the school. She mustn't wonder if Binh attended.

"Here at the equator the sun is extra bright," Di replied.

When they'd passed the white walls and headed toward the river, Binh let go of Di's hand to wipe her palm on her dress.

The procession crossed a foot bridge. Below, the river bubbled ferociously. The bridge was narrow and everyone crowded together, making Binh aware of the unfamiliar American scent of Di's skin.

On the other side of the river, with bamboo and big-leafed bushes growing thickly on either side, the path led up a small hill. Pebbles rolled underfoot. The sounds of the traffic grew distant.

Binh looked up to see the ancestors' house at the top of the hill, outlined against the sky. Painted a dull yellow, it was the size of her own house.

A blue dragon made of broken bottles and bits of smashed plates extended across the front wall.

As she and Di Thao and Ba Ngoai drew closer — all panting a little — Binh smelled the sweetness of the jasmine bush by the doorway.

Ba Ngoai stopped, putting her face close to the white jasmine flowers, breathing in deeply. "The ancestors live in this house," she said. "Just as we have a home, they must too."

Di snapped a photo and the yellow house magically appeared on the screen.

Inside the open doorway sat a small table with a flickering candle and a bundle of incense. Binh lit a stick. "You do the same," she whispered to Di.

The air was soon full of sweet smoke.

Di coughed.

Ma arranged the star fruit on the altar, then took the bananas from Anh Hai, the lilies from Ba Ngoai. She placed the offerings in front of the photographs of the ancestors.

Ba Ngoai knelt to bow three times, touching her forehead to the floor.

When Di bowed, she bent her neck to the side to

peek at the others. When she got up, she tripped on the hem of her dress.

The procession followed them home again. Another feast was being prepared, and the guests sat down once more along the table under the tree.

Binh went to the kitchen to help Ma with the cold coconut dessert soup. When she came out, she spotted Cuc sitting close to Di.

Cuc had held out her wrist and Di was examining Cuc's bracelets one by one. Surely, Di would see the bracelets looked just like the one she'd been given. She'd think Cuc had given it to her. Which was true.

"Your mother's looking for you," Binh said, coming up behind them.

Cuc's narrow eyes grew narrower. "You said that before. But she wasn't."

"Well, she looked like she was looking. . . ."

Cuc held out her other wrist to Di.

"Binh, Cuc! Come help!" Ma called out.

Binh smiled. Ma had chosen just the right moment.

"Carry out the soup, please, girls."

Cuc got up slowly, leaving her hand in Di's until the last second.

Binh lifted the clay pot by one handle, Cuc by the other. They had to move with care. Binh imagined letting go. Cuc would stumble and the sweet coconut would splash her polka-dotted dress.

They set the pot on the long table near Di.

"I just *love* all this Vietnamese food!" Di was saying to Second Uncle. "It reminds me of when I was a little girl."

"Then why aren't you eating any of the raw vegetables?" Second Uncle asked, tucking his beard out of the way.

"I . . ." Di began, her cheeks suddenly red. "When someone isn't used to the food, it can cause stomach problems."

"You must try the eel. It's very tasty." Second Uncle slipped a strip onto Di's plate.

Di dropped a pill into her glass of drinking water. The water turned yellow.

"Your water looks dirty," Cuc said over Di's shoulder.

Di laughed. "The pill is iodine. It kills the germs."

"But *we've* never gotten sick from the water," Second Uncle commented.

"You're used to it," Di said, swirling the water as the pill dissolved.

Binh glanced around. If the other relatives saw Di's dirty-looking water, they would whisper again. She frowned at Cuc, as if daring her to tell the secret.

"In America," Di said, "our water is very clean."

Binh stood where Di could see her. She looked longingly at the sky where the planes to America flew. "America sounds more and more wonderful. I wish I could go there."

"Maybe someday you will," Di answered.

Binh stirred the dirt with her toe. *Maybe. Someday.* Di hadn't said, *Don't worry, little niece. I will take you.*

Chapter Eleven

That night, lying next to Binh, Di tossed on her mat.

"Aren't you comfortable?" Binh asked.

Di sighed and tossed again. "I'm just not sleepy. I live on the other side of the world, Binh. The sun is shining there. My body still tells me that it's daytime, not time for sleep."

Binh tried to imagine living on the other side of the world. People would be standing upside down.

"Then tell me about the war," Binh whispered. "Tell me everything you remember."

Di sighed in the darkness. "I hardly remember anything. I was so young. I forced myself to forget."

"But you used to live here. . . ."

Di turned so her face was close to Binh's. "Okay. I remember the smells of the food cooking, the plants and trees. The soft feel of the air. But I don't have many memories of things happening. The only thing I remember is when I had to leave Ma, when the people took me away from her." Di grew silent.

"Tell me about that," Binh demanded.

Di sighed. "I remember the man taking me out of my mother's arms and into the airplane. It didn't have seats like most airplanes. Inside there was just a big dark space with crying children. I know now it was not a place for people to travel in. It was where they usually put cargo. Not children."

Binh leaned up on her elbow. Were the others sleeping or listening?

"When they shut the door, I saw Ma for the last time. She was crying and waving."

Ba Ngoai tossed on her mat.

A lump grew in Binh's throat, as if she'd swallowed a mango seed.

"I missed her, Binh, I missed her," Di whispered in Binh's ear.

In the bushes, the crickets began their nightly song.

"Good night, Di Hai," Binh whispered back. For once, she'd heard enough. She listened for her own ma's breathing and scooted a little closer.

"Do you think she will really take us to America?" Binh asked Ba Ngoai as they carried bowls of rice flavored with fish sauce to the dogs.

"Not right away. Arrangements would have to be made," Ba Ngoai answered, setting down the bowls. "I wouldn't go. I couldn't leave my home here."

Binh thought of Ba Ngoai combing her hair when she was small, mending her blue dress, giving her a packet of red hair ribbons last Lunar New Year. "Oh, Ba Ngoai, you have to come!"

Ba Ngoai shook her head.

Binh's heart contracted like a flower closing at sunset. She kicked at the ground. "And the dogs, could they go?"

Ba Ngoai laughed. "They would stay with me." She laid her hand on Binh's shoulder. "I don't think Thao has plans to take anyone."

"We'll see," Binh answered. Her foot moved close to a bowl of food and a dog nipped at her sandal.

Binh peeked into the kitchen, with its black walls and orange fire, to see Di and Ba Ngoai squatting side by side while they sliced vegetables into the soup. Their shoulders touched.

The kitchen cat slept by the fire.

Holding up a sprig of herb, Ba Ngoai said, "This is good for the stomach." She held up another. "This for a cough." She looked up and saw Binh. "Come in, *chau,* little granddaughter. You can teach your auntie to grind spices."

Binh squatted close to Di Thao and took the mortar and pestle from the low shelf. She dropped a handful of dried red chili into the stone bowl and pounded it with the cylindrical pestle.

"Let me try," said Di.

When the chili had been ground to a smooth powder, Di shook it into the soup.

The soup simmered, then boiled, and Ba Ngoai moved it to the edge of the flames. Then, tilting her head, trying to look into Di's face, she asked, "Was it hard for you in America, *con*?"

Binh settled back for a story.

Di fiddled with the hem of her T-shirt and said nothing.

"Was it hard?" Ba Ngoai repeated.

Di let go of the shirt and said slowly, "At first . . . at first America was very hard."

Hard? Binh hadn't expected to hear that. "How was it hard, Di Hai?" she asked. "Was it all that gunfire?"

"Oh, no." Di laughed briefly. "It was hard being an Asian child with white parents. Thirty years ago there weren't many Vietnamese in the southern part of the United States. I looked so different from my parents." She wiped her eyes with the back of her hand. "Everyone always knew that I was adopted. They felt sorry for me. I hated being different from the others."

Binh thought of how she too felt different when the schoolchildren came by her stand. But it was hard to imagine her auntie feeling left out and pitied in the heaven of America.

"Oh, Thao, I'm so sorry," said Ba Ngoai.

In the silence, the cat stretched, unfurled its pink tongue, and fell back asleep.

"Until coming here," Di sniffed, "I didn't understand how anyone could give me up."

"She had to . . ." Binh began, but Ba Ngoai frowned and said, "But now you understand?"

"I do. Life is hard here. And thirty years ago it was even harder. . . ."

"Yes, dear Thao."

"In America, I wasn't Vietnamese anymore," Di said so quietly that Binh had to hold her breath to hear. "And I didn't feel American either. I didn't belong in America. I had a hard time."

Binh thought of Vuong, who was also not Vietnamese or American. Vuong was never invited into anyone's house. When he delivered water, some people threw money at his feet instead of putting it in his hand.

As silence fell over the kitchen again, Binh uncrossed and crossed her legs. Would life be hard for *her* in America? Would she, like Di Hai, not feel like an American?

The soup began to smell of sweet, hot spices.

"And now I don't belong here either," Di said, her words like bruised flowers. "Here in Vietnam, I'm not Vietnamese. I'm not anything."

You're bui doi, Binh thought. *Less than dust.*

Di suddenly started to cry. "Why did you give me up, Ma?" Her eyes closed, the tears trickling out, she reached for Ba Ngoai. "I wanted *you.*"

Ba Ngoai held Di then, tiny against the giant child in her arms.

Binh stood up and slipped past them. Di Thao's words confused her. Although there was a lot of shooting in America, no movie had ever shown life there as so sad.

At Binh's sudden movement, the cat leaped up and darted outside.

Binh and Di Hai walked up the hill to the ancestral house, alone this time with no procession following them.

In her pocket Binh carried a small bottle of glue. She also carried a *ganh hang,* the bamboo pole across her shoulders, each dangling a bucket full of water.

"Oh, let me," Di had said, but Binh had insisted. She was used to carrying the water. Plus, the ancestors expected it of her.

As Binh walked, the water slapped the sides of the buckets.

At the top of the hill, faced with the yellow house and with the quiet spreading around them, they paused.

Binh wondered if the ancestors were confused by Di. Did they almost know who she was, but not quite? Were they scratching their heads?

Binh set down the *ganh hang* and followed Di into the ancestral house.

When Binh's eyes had grown used to the dark interior, she lit a stick of incense. She removed the wilting purple lilies from the vase. The tiny bananas and star fruit, once offered, had been eaten by the living.

As the incense unwound into a sweet cloud, Binh knelt and bowed. She sensed Di mimicking her, her forehead greeting the dusty floor.

Outside again, Binh emptied the two buckets of water onto the jasmine bush.

Di picked off a few loose, dried blossoms.

"And now," Binh said, shaking the last drops from the second bucket, "we need to look along the base of the wall for bits of the dragon. Pieces keep falling off." She held up a blue and white shard.

"Why, that looks like a dinner plate," Di exclaimed.

"It is. Look here." Binh pointed to the dragon's mane, made entirely out of broken ceramic soup spoons.

"How clever," Di said. "I wouldn't have noticed from far away. But up close . . ."

They hunted for the fallen bits and matched their findings with the bare spots on the wall.

"Tell me more about America," Binh said, squeezing the glue bottle with both hands while Di held the bit of plate. "Do people wear fancy clothes there, or do they wear old jeans?"

"People wear everything in America: ball gowns, cowboy boots, Indian saris," Di said, pressing the piece, dripping with glue, to the wall. "There are all kinds of people."

"Do *you* ever wear fancy clothes?"

"Not if I can help it!"

"You don't want to?"

"Don't want to. Can't afford to."

"But in America, isn't everyone rich?"

Di laughed. "Oh my, no! You've been watching too many movies!"

Binh picked up a very large shard and didn't answer.

This time, Di applied the glue. "And now let me

ask *you* a question," she said when the piece was coated white. "Your family has very little space. You're almost sleeping on top of each other. Yet there's this whole empty house. Couldn't the ancestors share?" Di reached to her full height to press the piece onto the wall.

Binh sucked in her breath and glanced toward the dark doorway. Had the ancestors heard Di? Were they murmuring among themselves? Were they saying that Di had a huge house with no room for them, yet had suggested that *they* share?

"Without ancestors, we wouldn't be alive," Binh said. "They deserve a place of their own."

Di shook her head as though she still didn't understand. The fragment dropped and Di recovered it. She stood tall, pushing it firmly.

And yet it was hard to blame Di for not having a connection to her ancestors, Binh thought. By going to America, she'd been cut off from them. Her new American parents wouldn't have known who they were. Maybe the parents didn't even care.

And then Binh had a troubling thought. If she went to America, her ancestors would be, like Di's, left behind here in Vietnam. She would lose her connection to them, their protection.

If she went away, it would be like cutting herself off from a living, growing, green vine. The small branch that she was would wilt, like the lilies she'd thrown out onto the ground.

If she went to America, someone else would water the ancestors' jasmine bush. Someone else would repair the dragon.

Slowly, Di released her fingers. The piece stuck.

Chapter Twelve

 Three days went by.

Cuc brought Di a frog—eyes popping—made of shells. When Binh examined the frog, she found a small chip on one of the shells. The knickknack was probably a reject from the shop.

Ba and Anh Hai used their dragons as doorstops.

Binh, Ma, and Ba Ngoai laid their stone hearts on the ancestral altar.

Di took photos of the pink dragons, the tree, the river, the inside and outside of the house from every angle, every relative who came by.

Sometimes she let Binh use the camera, showing her how to look through the tiny window and telling her when to push the button. Binh photographed mostly the ducks and dogs.

In the morning, Di brought out her paper and colored pencils. Binh watched, fascinated at the way stands of bamboo, the swirling river, Fourth Aunt, and a duck taking a bath came alive on Di's paper.

As they sat by the river, Di said, "None of my greens are bright enough for this jungle." She motioned toward the banana trees and bamboo, and the tangle of vines connecting them.

Sometimes Di drew pictures of things that Binh was unfamiliar with: a box that carried people up and down inside a building, a house with wheels pulled behind a car.

Once when Di was putting away her paper and colored pencils, she glanced toward Binh's fruit cart, parked against the side of the house. "That's cute. What's it for?"

Binh pretended to peer at the cart. "I don't know. Maybe it belongs to Ba's cousin." Why did Di have to notice the cart? She must never know that Binh sold fruit and sodas instead of going to school. Tonight, Binh promised herself, she would cover up the cart so that Di wouldn't be reminded of it.

When Vuong delivered the water, Di Thao chatted with him. She took his picture and invited him to drink tea with her under the big tree.

Maybe Di Thao would marry Vuong and take him to America.

"Vuong is *bui doi*," Binh said to Di once after Vuong had brought the water.

"*Less than dust.* What an awful thing to say! Why don't the Vietnamese like people with American fathers?"

"Because those people don't really belong to Vietnam. They can't be buried properly here. They will never be honored by their ancestors."

Di looked puzzled. "Why is that, Binh?"

"Because their American ancestors were those of the invaders. How can anyone trust an invader?"

"That's nonsense," said Di. "Vuong is not an invader. And I am not either."

"Oh, I didn't mean . . ." Binh began.

Di interrupted. "On my first day of school in Kentucky, I didn't speak English. I couldn't understand anything the teacher or other kids were saying."

Sometimes at Café Video, Binh closed her eyes to the subtitles and just listened to the English. She quickly grew frustrated and opened her eyes again. How would it be to listen to those nonsense sounds all day?

"Yet I wasn't Vietnamese anymore either," Di went on. "I had new American parents. I had nothing left of Vietnam. That felt very bad. And Vuong's life is like that. Not one thing, not another."

Binh stared at the ground. She thought of the way some women shouted at Vuong when he brought water.

Every afternoon, the other relatives came by the house, wanting to see Di Thao, to sit close to her, to be favored by her.

Di listened to the conversations, her forehead

wrinkled as she tried to understand. "What are they saying?" she often asked Binh.

And Binh would explain. Instead of telling stories, Di kept asking questions.

The older women sat around the big table, rolling a white paste into green areca palm leaves. When they chewed the little package, their mouths and teeth turned dark red.

"Their teeth are almost black," Di said.

"Don't old women in America want beautiful teeth?"

"Are dark red teeth *beautiful*?"

"Of course."

Di laughed. "A lot of Americans have teeth made of plastic."

It was Binh's turn to laugh. She'd never heard of such a thing as plastic teeth. Better to have no teeth at all!

Some of the men played *tam cuc,* a kind of poker game, while the smoke of their cigarettes rose into the air above them. Some read newspapers from Ho Chi Minh City.

In the afternoons, everyone laid out sleeping mats under the tree and napped.

※　※　※

Ba and Anh Hai returned to work. After all, Di Hai was one more mouth to feed.

Third Aunt returned to her tourist shop, taking Cuc with her, commenting, "Even though she's American, that woman doesn't know how to be a good guest."

And Ba said, "Binh, your auntie hasn't made us rich, after all. Soon you need to return to the fruit cart."

Chapter Thirteen

One morning, Di lifted the blue plastic off the fruit cart. "Oh," she said, "I was hoping to use this tarp, but I see it's protecting this."

"Don't worry," said Binh. "That old cart will be okay."

"Then take one end, please."

Binh held the plastic—what was Auntie up to now?—while Di stretched it out and tied it to the base of the tree.

"Now up here," Di said, yanking the rope on the other end until it reached the bathroom roof. She tied the corners of the tarp onto the nails that stuck out.

Di stepped inside the new enclosure. Although she had to crouch because of the low ceiling, she said, "This makes a good sleeping room."

"A sleeping room?" Binh asked as a breeze rippled the blue ceiling. This didn't look like the rooms that Di had shown in her photographs.

"I need privacy. I'm not used to sleeping with so many people."

Binh thought of the mats laid side by side. She'd never thought it strange to sleep in the same room as her family. She liked feeling everyone around her. Family kept the ghosts at bay.

Now Di was moving away from them, to live outside like the ducks and dogs. There would be no more whispered late-night stories.

"Do you want me to go away, then?" Binh's voice trembled.

"Don't be upset." Di put an arm around her shoulders. "I'm still close by."

"You won't be afraid of the ghosts?" Binh asked.

Di threw back her head and laughed.

"Isn't our house good enough for her?" Ma asked after Di had retired to her little hut, her *cai coc.*

"Doesn't she like us?" asked Anh Hai.

"In the photographs, you can see she has a lot more rooms in America," said Ba Ngoai.

"Enough for all of us," said Ma.

"Enough for the whole village," said Ba.

The four voices wound in and out of each other.

"She thinks she is too good for us."

"But she is sleeping on the *dirt.*"

"She doesn't like us." Ma pulled the *non la* frame close to her and prepared to work.

"Let me sew a little, Ma," Binh said.

Ma made room for Binh. As Binh plunged the sharp needle over and over into the soft straw, she thought of the morning when she'd first laid out Di Thao's sleeping mat next to her own. She thought of how now, instead of being closer to her auntie, she was farther away.

Why didn't Di Hai want to be close to them? Binh

poked the needle hard and accidentally pricked her finger.

Binh was sweeping the yard, raising small clouds of dust, scooting aside the ducks with the broom.

Anh Hai sat on a bench, digging out the white meat from a coconut shell. "Aren't you and Cuc close anymore?" he asked.

Binh shrugged and kept on sweeping.

"You're always chasing her away from Di Hai."

Binh sent a flurry of dust in Anh Hai's direction.

"It's not like there's much to be jealous of," Anh Hai continued, ignoring the dust, scooping deeper into the coconut. "If only she'd take us to America. There's nicer motorcycles there."

"She still might," Binh protested. How could Anh Hai give up so easily?

"Don't count on it. Our auntie didn't give us much of anything."

"She still might," Binh repeated.

"She won't. She doesn't understand us."

Binh leaned on the handle of the broom. "Maybe she's saving something for later. In her suitcase. That's why she moved to the *cai coc*. So we wouldn't see."

"I dare you to look then," Anh Hai said. He tossed a bite of coconut to a duck.

"In her *suitcase*?"

"If that's where you think the treasure lies."

"But that's . . ."

"You're not brave enough."

"Fine," said Binh, flicking the tail of a duck with the broom. She glanced toward the kitchen. The smell of *pho bo,* traditional Vietnamese noodle soup, drifted from the doorway. Ba Ngoai and Di were cooking together, chopping and talking of the past. Right now, nothing else existed for them.

With Anh Hai on the bench keeping watch, Binh crawled into the *cai coc*. The light inside was blue and dim. She knelt in front of the suitcase and lifted the lid.

She heard a noise and listened, her heart hammering. But the sound was that of Anh Hai whistling to himself. There were no footsteps.

She found clothes, a bag. She touched the bag and discovered the outline of a pair of shoes.

She stuck her hand in the side pockets. A comb. A book. Di's photo book. Four pairs of socks.

Binh sat back on her heels. Was this all there was to her auntie? Was she really so simple? Was she nothing like what Binh had seen in the movies?

Where *was* the jewelry? The small, precious items? Was Anh Hai right?

Binh closed the suitcase.

Finding nothing was like watching the morning mist disappear when the sun rose.

As Binh crawled out, Anh Hai called, "I see your pockets are heavy with treasure."

Binh picked up the broom and swatted him on the shins.

"Ouch," Anh Hai cried, throwing down the empty coconut.

Binh swatted him again, this time pretending he was Di Hai.

Then she dropped the broom and walked out of the yard. She marched down the highway along its narrow shoulder, as cars and trucks honked.

It took her an hour to reach Third Aunt's tourist shop.

The shop was a small hut where the highway intersected the road to the beach. Each day, a few cars stopped with customers. If Third Aunt was lucky, a tour bus would pull in, leaving the engine roaring, the fumes filling the shop.

Binh found Cuc kneeling to unpack a small box.

As she stepped close, Cuc's hands grew still, but she didn't look up. "Your auntie go home?"

"Not yet."

"Then why are you here?"

Binh squatted down, the box with its loose newspaper between them. She glimpsed ashtrays made of coconut shells in the wrapping. "I searched Di Hai's suitcase."

Cuc let her hands rest on the edge of the box. "And?" she asked.

"There was nothing in it except her clothes and a few other things."

"Isn't that what you expected?"

Binh straightened a piece of newspaper. What *had* she expected? The ink from the newsprint smudged her fingers. She'd searched a guest's suitcase all for nothing. Now she felt smudged inside, too.

"I'm not sure," she finally said.

Cuc continued the unpacking, setting the ashtrays on a low shelf behind her.

"Do you want help?" Binh asked.

"I can do it," Cuc replied. Then, a round ashtray in her hands, she said casually, "Even though Di Hai isn't such a close relative to me as she is to you, I think she means to take me to America."

Binh crumpled the bit of newspaper, fingernails biting into her palm. "What do you mean?"

"I'm a year older than you. It would be easier for

her to take just me." She pulled herself up. "I'm old enough to go without my family."

Binh threw the wad of paper back into the box. She'd never imagined . . . This couldn't be! "Has Di Hai said anything?"

Cuc cocked her head to the side. "Not in words. But I can tell."

Chapter Fourteen

Binh ran all the way home from Third Aunt's shop, stopping only once to splash her face with river water.

She found Di in the yard, washing her hair. She stood with her feet wide over a red basin, her head a mass of white foam.

That red basin was for washing vegetables, not hair. Di should be using the *green* one. If Ma came along, she'd be upset.

Binh pretended not to see the color of the basin. "Di, Di Hai." She sank down, breathless from her run.

Di scooped water with a cup, rinsing out the soap.

It wasn't a good moment to bring up anything important, but Binh couldn't wait. She had to act before

Di and Cuc made plans. "We would like to go to America with you, Di Hai," she said loudly so that Di could hear over the washing. "Just my close family. Just four of us. Ba Ngoai doesn't want to go." *Or Cuc, either,* she felt like adding.

Di kept rinsing.

Binh leaned down, trying to see the expression on Di's face.

"Oh, darn, now I have soap in my eyes," Di said. "Binh, do me a favor and throw out this soapy water. Get me some fresh."

Binh threw the soapy water across the yard. In the bathroom, she dipped clean water into the red basin. Why wouldn't Di answer her?

Di finished rinsing her hair and wrapped it up in a towel. With the cone of towel on top of her head, she looked taller than ever. "Now, what's this you're asking?"

"We'd like to go with you to America," Binh repeated.

"*What?*" Di asked again. Water ran down the sides of her face.

"We want to live with you."

Di slapped her hand to her forehead. "You've been thinking about that all this time? That I'd wave a wand and you'd all be in Kentucky?"

"Oh, no. You would make arrangements," Binh said, remembering Ba Ngoai's explanation.

"You must think I'm magic." The towel came loose and fell around Di's shoulders. "I am a small, unimportant person. I have not much money, no power . . . I never dreamed you expected such a thing."

Once Binh had been running and had fallen onto her chest, knocking the breath out of her. Now, too, she could scarcely breathe.

"You don't understand what it would mean to go to America," Di went on. "You don't know what you'd be leaving behind." She rubbed her red eyes—irritated by the soap—with the corner of the towel.

"But you said it was a good thing to go," Binh persisted. "That your new mother gave you a better life."

Di squeezed her eyes shut. "That soap was so strong." She sat down on the bench.

Binh felt as though she'd gotten soap in her own eyes.

After a while, Di said, "Binh . . . I'm sorry. I didn't know. . . . Sit here." She patted a spot beside her on the bench.

Binh sat, but not as close as Di indicated.

Di sighed. "My situation wasn't the same as yours. When I left, this country was at war. Children like me were being killed. You're not in danger." She began to dry her hair, rubbing it with quick, circular movements.

Suddenly, Binh stood up. "You shouldn't have used that red basin. You should put it back on the shelf."

Di paused, one hand holding the towel to her head.

Binh picked up the basin and waved it, startling the ducks. "We can never use this to wash vegetables again."

The towel dropped onto Di's shoulders. "I'm sorry. I didn't know. I'll buy you another. Don't worry. I'll . . . I'll buy you several."

Binh slapped the empty basin against the side of the

big table. The table creaked and the last suds flew out. "You didn't come here to buy us plastic basins. That's not what we expected of you."

Di started to stand, then sat back down.

Binh put her hands on her hips and asked, "Are you going to take Cuc to America?"

Di sighed again and laid the towel on the bench. "Of course not."

Just then, Binh saw Ma standing under the arch of pink and white bougainvillea, Ba Ngoai behind her like a small shadow. They'd overheard everything.

Binh didn't know whether to hold the red basin out to Ma as evidence, or whether to hide it behind her back. She threw it onto the ground behind her, where it rolled under the table.

Di's eyes followed Binh's gaze to the archway. She managed to stand. "It takes a lot of money to bring relatives to America." She held out her empty hands. "I'm not rich." She closed her hands, hiding her lack.

Ma and Ba Ngoai just stared, their faces unchanged.

When Binh looked at the two framed by the arch, she couldn't imagine them anyplace but there, poised between the bustle of the highway and the sleepy flow of the river.

Ba Ngoai didn't want to go to America anyway, Binh recalled. And Ma? Ma only wanted money for this and that.

Binh took a step backward. Had she been the only one with such hopes?

"My little niece," Di continued, "has many distorted ideas about the United States. It is not a place where everyone is rich and happy. Not at all. Binh is better off here."

Ba Ngoai stepped in front of Ma. A bougainvillea flower dropped onto her shoulder as she left the safety of the arch. She crossed the yard quickly and laid a hand on Di's arm. "You, my daughter, are here as our guest. We expect nothing of you."

Ma leaned against the frame of the arch, just watching, her eyes narrowed.

Binh strode toward Ma, on her way out of the yard for the second time that day.

But when she drew close, Ma took her by the arm. "Binh! How could you have spoken to Di Hai like that?"

Binh looked at the ground and sighed. Ma just didn't understand.

"You have been watching too many American movies, *con*. You have lost your gentle Vietnamese manners."

Ma let go, yet Binh still felt the pressure of Ma's strong fingers against her flesh. She went out of the yard and off down the highway, rubbing her arm. This time, there was nowhere to run to but the motorcycle repair shop.

"Nev-er. Nev-er. Nev-er," she chanted in time with her footsteps. Never again would she ask Di Hai for anything. And, no matter what Ma said, Di didn't deserve to be treated with nice manners.

Now she would not sit, even in the back row, of Di Hai's classroom. She wouldn't sleep in Di's lacy guest bed or zip along the ocean in a fast car. She wouldn't ever eat her fill of French fries and milk shakes. Worst of all, she'd never see the world beyond this tiny village.

A bus honked, startling her. Binh shook her fist at the driver.

A layer of grease, uneven and black, spread over the floor of the repair shop. Binh glimpsed Anh Hai inside, siphoning gas from an engine into soda cans. Ba sat with two other men smoking in the back.

Binh realized that if Ba saw her out in the street with nothing to do, he'd remember the fruit cart.

She walked home slowly, scuffing at the dirt with her sandals.

School was over for the day and as Binh passed the school gate, she stopped and looked through the bars.

A woman wearing a white *ao dai* crossed the courtyard with a stack of books. She glanced in Binh's direction and for a moment—could it be?—Binh fancied that the woman smiled at her.

Chapter Fifteen

*E*arly the next morning, Binh found Ba Ngoai outside in the *cai coc*. Kneeling beside Di, she sponged her face with a damp cloth.

"She's feverish," Ba Ngoai whispered.

"Oh, no," Binh whispered back. Had Di gotten sick from eating a raw vegetable? Had she drunk water without purifying it?

"Binh," said Ba Ngoai, "please get me another cool wet cloth. Send Hai to the village for herbs. Tell Ba to light incense at the ancestral house."

"What about a doctor?" Di asked, her voice as pale as her face.

"There is no doctor in this village. Van can bring a monk from the temple."

Binh went inside with the news: "Di Hai is very sick with a bad stomach."

Anh Hai and Ba rode off on the borrowed motorcycle, Ma sandwiched between them.

Over and over, Ba Ngoai dipped the cloth in a basin of water, wrung it out, and placed it on Di's burning forehead.

Suddenly, Di cried out, "Ma! Ma!" and clung to Ba Ngoai. "I was outside with other children. We were playing war, each of us carrying a large stick of bamboo, shooting each other. One boy wouldn't play dead. We heard a sound in the sky. You came running out of the house shouting at us to get inside."

Di pulled the blanket around her and trembled.

The fever had reawakened Di's war memories. Binh listened, her hand pressed to her heart.

Outside, a bird gave a long, wild cry.

Di gazed at the blue plastic sky of the *cai coc* as though looking into the sky of long ago. "We ran inside when heaven fell. The earth shook. When all quieted, we went out. The neighbor's water buffalo was dead . . . And old Mr. Trinh . . . And the little boy I'd shot dead during our game. He hadn't run fast enough." Di began to sob.

Ba Ngoai pulled both Di and Binh close to her, trying to encircle them with her tiny arms. "Shhh . . ." she said.

Binh found her cheek against Di's shoulder.

"Sometimes," Di said, her voice like dried leaves underfoot, "I wonder if instead of running as he should have, that boy was playing dead for me."

A tear ran down the side of Binh's face. Nothing in her own life had ever been that sad.

When Di lay back down, Binh took the cooling cloth from Ba Ngoai and sponged Di Hai's forehead herself.

That afternoon, two Buddhist nuns came to the house to perform a ceremony for the sick, burning incense and chanting: "May your heart's garden bloom with a thousand lotus flowers. . . ."

The air smelled of the bitter herbs brewing over the cooking fire.

Ba Ngoai gave Di a healing massage, rubbing oil into her back with the flat side of a spoon. She pressed so hard that Di cried out.

When Anh Hai started to crack open a coconut, Ma said, "That sound is too loud for your auntie," and Anh Hai set his big knife aside.

Cuc brought a cold can of artichoke soda.

"You should stay away from my auntie," Binh said, dipping the cloth. "You might catch what she has."

Just after sunrise, Binh took Di a steaming bowl of *pho bo*.

Di sat up, swallowed a spoonful, and smiled. "I can feel the soup landing in my stomach. I think it'll stay there this time."

Binh settled down, her back against the suitcase.

Di ate until the bowl was empty. Then, setting the bowl aside, said, "While I was sick, I thought about what you asked about. I feel terrible about getting your hopes up."

Binh bit the inside of her cheek.

Di leaned forward. "I'm so sorry."

Binh shook her head slightly, not trusting herself to speak.

"I can't take you to America, but how about a short trip away from here?" Di said. "We could go somewhere nice."

Binh gave Di a little smile.

"In the suitcase behind you, there's a book. Why don't you get it out."

Binh opened the suitcase as though unfamiliar with it. She knew right where Di kept the book, but pretended to search. "This one?" The cover read *Vietnam.*

Di held out her hand. "I'm not doing the touristy things I thought I'd be doing."

As Di flipped through the pages, Binh saw Vietnamese women in traditional dress wearing flowers in their hair, monks and nuns holding alms bowls, a pond of pink lotus blooms. Finally, Di turned to a picture of the ocean, turquoise and glittering under the sun.

"Oh!" Binh exclaimed.

"Haven't you seen the ocean?"

Binh shook her head. "Only in movies."

"Have you never traveled beyond your village, Binh?" Di asked gently.

Binh set down the guidebook. "Once Anh Hai took me on a motorcycle, up the highway to the tea plantations."

"Well, it's time you saw more than tea. Let's go to the beach," Di said. "We could take a bus."

Binh gripped the book with both hands. "Could we really go? Could we go in the ocean?" She didn't know how to swim, but loved to kneel down in the river, the water up to her shoulders.

"Of course we'll swim. Let's see, it says here that the closest beach is about a three-hour drive. There are several hotels and restaurants."

"I'll ask Ma if we can go." Binh scrambled to her feet.

"Ask if we can go tomorrow!" Di called after her.

Binh hesitated. Suddenly, she wanted to ask if Cuc could come too. Like Binh, Cuc had never been to the ocean. But then Binh recalled the way Cuc had shown off her bracelets. What else would Cuc show off to Auntie? Saying nothing, Binh left the *cai coc*.

Chapter Sixteen

The next morning, as stars still shone in the sky, half the village turned out to watch Di Thao and Binh board the early bus for the beach town of Mui Ne. The bus picked up passengers from the side of the highway. It was bigger than Binh's house, and as it waited for the new passengers, it rumbled like an angry dragon.

Ma pressed two baguette sandwiches into Binh's hands. "You may find only very bad food."

Ba and Anh Hai wore their best shirts in honor of this special good-bye. The white cotton glowed in the dim light.

This time, Binh thought, it was she and not Anh Hai who was leaving.

Ba Ngoai held Di's hand. "You'll be gone so long, dear daughter."

"Only a day."

"But I will miss you terribly."

Binh put Ma's food in the plastic bag with the two towels and a small woven mat. She and Di each carried one of Ma's *non la*s as protection from the sun.

The morning was lit with the flash from Di's camera.

For a moment there in the morning dark, on the known stretch of highway, surrounded by familiar faces, including those of the street mongrels, Binh shivered with a sudden sadness. Maybe she didn't want to go to the ocean, after all. She'd left her village only once before, and then had been on the back of the motorcycle, snuggled against Anh Hai for protection.

"It's time," Di said, taking Binh by the elbow.

Binh waved good-bye to Cuc. Even now it wasn't too late to ask Di. But Binh turned away, her face wooden and set, like the carved animals in Third Aunt's shop.

Two birds began to sing as Binh, aware of the many

eyes watching her, climbed the silver steps into the bus. The interior hummed and vibrated. She steadied herself by holding the rail that ran close to the ceiling.

"Sit here," said Di, stopping by two seats. "Close to the front, we won't smell that awful smoke."

As the bus chugged off, the driver leaning out his window to yell at a man on a large tricycle, Binh pulled aside the curtain and waved to her family standing in a neat line. Their faces looked small and blurry on the other side of the window glass.

When they turned at the road to the beach, Binh saw Third Aunt's tourist shop, closed and dark in this early hour. Later on, instead of playing in the ocean, Cuc would set the coconut ashtrays to one side, dust the shelf, and move the ashtrays back.

The bus ascended into the hills. In the pale silver light, Binh made out the tea plants Anh Hai had once shown her, their rows curving over the folds of the earth.

As the sky lightened, they drove through one village after another. Each flew the same red and yellow banners of the Communist party, while the Buddhist flags waved from the pagodas.

When the hillsides flattened out, the villages grew larger. Huge balconies protruded from the second stories of the houses. On some balconies stood statues of the Virgin Mary holding out her arms to the world. Binh had never seen such large statues—only the tiny ones in Third Aunt's shop.

Binh held the plastic bag with Ma's food close to her. She had wanted to see the world. But Di was taking her so far away. Maybe Di had been right about America. By going, she would leave too much behind.

As in her village, Binh saw piles of burning trash, the smoke thickening the air. Men and women squatted by the side of the road next to huge piles of fruits and vegetables, stacked baskets, turquoise sacks of rice, and tall stalks of bright flowers.

Midmorning, the bus stopped at a roadside restaurant with one wall open to the highway. When the bus door opened, a gang of children holding bundles of postcards pressed close.

They began to call out to Di: "Madame! Madame!"

Di examined a display of cards carried by a small boy with a dirty bandanna around his head.

The boy winked at his friend and gave a thumbs-up sign.

"I'll take three, please," Di finally said in Vietnamese, giving the boy a bill. She lifted her camera and snapped a picture of him.

He held out his hand.

"He wants more money because you took his picture," Binh explained.

"For just that?" Di protested, while laying another bill in the boy's open palm.

The other children moved in. "Madame! Madame!" They posed with big smiles and the girls flirted.

"You're so pretty. You're so handsome," Di exclaimed as she photographed them.

But to Binh, they looked dirty and greedy. Worse,

they pretended to like Di Thao, when all they wanted was her money.

Di took pictures of every one of them, then showed them the pictures on the camera screen. She handed out many small bills.

Binh pulled Di into the restaurant, calling out to the children, "Don't follow us!"

As she and Di sat down at a table, Binh said, "Those kids are overcharging you."

Di raised her eyebrows so high they rose over the top of her sunglasses.

Inside the open air restaurant, the driver and passengers bent over bowls of *pho bo*.

Di and Binh ate the baguettes Ma had sent—French bread stuffed with bean curd and greens—while the children watched from the edge of the restaurant.

"Madame, Madame," they called in soft voices.

Di bought flat round sheets of sesame candy and a box of candied ginger.

As they made their way back to the bus, the children

once again crowded around, shoving postcards toward Di Hai.

Di gave them the ginger, and the boy with the bandanna made a face.

"Go away," Binh said to the boy. "You've gotten enough out of her already."

Once back in the bus, Di waved at the children, then looked at the postcards. "My students will love seeing these." She took out her sketchbook and did quick drawings of the children until the bus pulled away.

Binh leaned close, even though she wished Di would draw something else.

Di put away her pencil and unwrapped the sesame candy. "I remember this candy from when I was a child. I'd forgotten it. I loved the way it stuck in my teeth, the tiny seeds . . ."

The towns came to an end and the bus passed into the jungle of bamboo, vines, and big-leafed trees.

The air whistling through the crack in the window smelled salty.

After they passed a gigantic Buddha perched

serenely on a boulder, the bus climbed over one last rise and the ocean lay at the base of the hills.

Binh pressed her face against the window. As the bus drew closer, she drew herself up, straining to comprehend the blue line of the horizon.

Chapter Seventeen

*T*he bus stopped. The doors fanned open to let Binh and Di Thao climb out into the salty, damp air.

There were no buildings, no street vendors—not even children selling postcards—in this deserted spot.

A small, dusty road lined with palm trees led to the ocean. As they walked, Di took many pictures and Binh heard an unfamiliar, restless roar. "What's that noise?"

Di stopped and listened. "It's the ocean."

The ocean sounded like the breathing of a giant monster, yet Di didn't seem worried.

They walked on down the road, the waves growing louder.

"Let's take off our sandals," Di said when the road ended at a mound of white sand.

Binh wiggled her feet as she walked, the sand warm and slippery between her toes. The sun shone like a huge, bare bulb in the sky. How nice it would be to plunge into the water!

Yet when she saw the ocean, it moved not in one direction like the river, but every which way. It pulled back in on itself and lunged forward. This was the huge, gobbling monster she'd imagined down the road, worse than any ghost.

Binh wasn't sure she wanted to go in after all. She might get lost in so much water.

Di took her dress off, revealing a red bathing suit underneath.

Binh didn't have on a suit. When she bathed in the river and no one was around, she wore her underwear. She hadn't thought of needing a bathing suit. If she didn't have one, would she not be able to swim? She poked her big toe into the hard, wet sand.

She pretended to be interested in the boys and older

women who pulled nets through the shallow water, collecting tiny butterfly shells.

Di asked gently, "You didn't bring a change of clothes, did you, Binh?"

Binh studied her bare feet.

Di looked around. "I don't see any shops here. Just swim in your dress and it'll dry."

Binh dropped her sandals and the plastic bag of their things onto the sand. Di expected her to go in the water. If she didn't, her auntie would be disappointed.

They waded into the warm water beside a man maneuvering a boat woven like a round basket. The ocean moved against Binh, pulling her one way, then another. She gripped Di's hand harder. The ocean might carry her to the horizon, which was a faraway, clear line— unlike the uneven horizon of the valley where she lived.

"Don't be afraid, Binh. This water is shallow. The waves aren't strong enough to hurt us."

Binh could see the bottom, crisscrossed by ripples of light.

Di took Binh's hand and led her in deeper, past the point where the man had climbed into his round boat, past where the waves pushed and pulled. Here the water rose gently, taking Binh up and down.

Di let go of her hand. "You're on your own now." She lay flat on her back, her suit very red in the turquoise water.

"I can't swim," Binh called out.

"You don't need to swim here. The water isn't deep," said Di, righting herself.

The round boat was small now, the man rowing out to sea using a palm leaf as an oar.

"Lie down, Binh. I'll hold you up."

Binh lay with Di supporting her. Her dress billowed around her and salty water splashed into her mouth. She coughed.

Di withdrew her hands and Binh continued to float. She rode on the surface of the ocean, the sun hot on her face, the outlines of her body disappearing.

After a while, Binh stood up. "Let me carry *you* in the water, Di."

Di threw herself back and allowed Binh to move her this way and that. Di weighed nothing!

If only Cuc were here, she suddenly thought. She thought of her now, perhaps flattening cardboard boxes for the recycler to collect.

Suddenly, Di stood up. "It's time to go."

"Oh, can't we stay longer? We just got here."

"I feel bad. Everyone was hoping to go to America." Di said, the blue-green of the ocean reflecting onto her face. "I'd like to make it up to them. I'd like to do some shopping."

Shopping! Binh's eyes grew wide.

Yet as she followed Di out of the water, Binh sighed and caressed the smooth waves. She might never be here again. Reluctantly, she stepped out of the white foam and onto the hard sand once again.

Di pulled her dress on over her wet bathing suit. "Your clothes will dry by the time we get to the main road."

As they walked across the mounds of warm sand,

Binh kept looking over her shoulder at the ocean. A wind had come up, flecking the blue water with white.

Binh leaned down and picked up a small pink shell. She put it in her pocket. The shell hadn't cost a thing. It wasn't American. But it was nonetheless beautiful.

Chapter Eighteen

The highway led into a town unlike any that Binh had seen. No one squatted by the side of the road selling flat baskets of fruit or vegetables. No shops sold car parts or machinery. No chickens meandered.

Instead, shop after shop sold tourist items: *non la*s with fancy paintings, paper fans with cut designs, carved animals, bowls made of coconut shells.

People with round eyes and all colors of hair—light brown, yellow, and even orange—strolled in and out of the shops. None spoke Vietnamese.

Binh stared at these people, who looked like the children in the photographs of Di Thao's school.

"Lots of foreigners here," Di merely commented.

Binh noticed that both Vietnamese and foreigners stared at Di.

Di stopped in front of a restaurant with a patio. Each table was sheltered by a brightly colored umbrella. "This looks like fun. Italian food will be a nice change from rice and vegetables."

The umbrellas were lit with strings of lanterns. Cheerful music played from the loudspeakers.

"Madame," a Vietnamese man said, then uttered some words in English.

Di spoke Vietnamese. "I am here with my niece for dinner."

The man raised his eyebrows and looked at Di more closely. He led them to a table and pulled out chairs for each of them.

Di read the menu, which was not in Vietnamese. "How about spaghetti, Binh? That's noodles—surely you'd like those—with red tomato sauce."

When the waiter came, a small white towel over his forearm, Di pointed to the menu. "Two of these dinners, please."

As they waited for food, Di took out her camera and they looked through the photos of the day: taking off in the bus, the photos of the street children ("I'd rather not look at *them*!" Binh protested), the road to the beach, the ocean.

Then Di took a photo of Binh drinking limeade there in the Italian restaurant.

The spaghetti arrived. The waiter also brought bread in a basket and small plates of salad.

When Binh tried to lift the slippery noodles with her spoon, they slid off. The waiter hadn't brought chopsticks.

"Like this," Di said. "Use this to move the noodles onto the spoon." She held up a silver tool that looked like what Ma used to turn the soil in the garden.

Binh picked up the unfamiliar tool and copied Di. But the strong-smelling cheese made her stomach queasy. The red sauce tasted sour and harsh. "Do they have food like this in America?" she asked.

"Oh, yes. People call it Italian food, but it's very popular in America."

Binh slowly moved the unfamiliar eating tool into the noodles.

When the waiter brought the check, Di glanced at it then pulled bill after bill from her wallet.

Binh stared at the pile of money Di put down. It had paid for just one meal for the two of them, yet it could have bought rice and vegetables forever and ever.

Leaving the restaurant, they walked down the street, past women and girls peddling cups of fruit, sodas, and coconuts. Binh thought of how soon she too would be selling by the side of the road.

They wandered into a shop many times bigger than Third Aunt's tourist shop. Binh gazed at shells with words painted on them, parasols like huge flowers, dolls wearing tiny *ao dai*s—while Di made her way to a rack of clothing at the rear of the shop.

"Look, Binh. They have dresses. Why don't we buy you something clean to change into?" Di pushed the dresses along the rod, pausing over some, fingering the fabric.

Binh lifted her eyes to the wall, where an *ao dai*

hung. The tunic was of apple green silk, the loose trousers white. The pattern on the green silk was like soft clouds. It wasn't American. But it was so lovely. . . .

Pointing to the *ao dai,* Di beckoned the shopkeeper.

The shopkeeper began to speak to Di in English. When Binh listened to English in movies, it sounded strange to her. But at least she had subtitles to read. Here there were no subtitles and she was lost in a sea of words.

In America it would be like that: a continuous noise like the rumble of the ocean, sounds that made no sense.

As Di and the woman spoke back and forth, Binh gazed up at the *ao dai.*

Finally, the woman used a long-handled hook to lower first the trousers, then the tunic.

"How much is it?" Binh asked Di.

"Three hundred thousand *dong.*"

Binh sucked in her breath. She sold cups of pineapple for one thousand *dong.* Three hundred thousand *dong* would buy a school uniform.

The shopkeeper led Binh behind a curtain, where

she changed out of her salty blue dress into the magnificent *ao dai*. The silk was cool against her skin, just as she'd always imagined. She fastened the soft loopy buttons and straightened the high-necked collar.

When she came out, the shopkeeper and Di both smiled.

"Look in the mirror, Binh," said Di. "You look beautiful now."

The mirror was as tall as Binh. She stood straighter and smoothed her hair, stringy with salt water, away from her face.

She felt her whole body cool in the silk. It was her special moment. Di was offering to buy her an *ao dai* even prettier than the ones the high-school girls wore. And yet . . . her heart didn't sing as she'd expected. Instead, it churned like a motor about to break.

How could she wear something that cost so much when Ma and Ba fretted about money?

Binh turned around, looking back over her shoulder once more, studying the elegant stranger she'd become, then returned to the dressing room.

"You can wear it home if you like," Di called.

But Binh undid the loopy buttons with heavy hands, her fingers clumsy. She hung the pants, then the tunic, back on the hangers, then slipped her salty blue dress over her head.

Stepping out, the dressing room curtain falling into place behind her, Binh handed the *ao dai* to her auntie. "I have no place to wear this."

Di straightened one trouser leg. "Not to a wedding?"

"It's not really that." She looked up at the ceiling. "It costs too much."

Di lowered her eyebrows and stared hard at Binh. "Before you said I didn't come here to buy you red plastic basins. . . ."

Binh blushed at the reminder.

"Are you now saying I shouldn't buy you a nice gift either?"

Binh looked down at her blue dress. A small hole had appeared near the waist. Soon the fabric would rot—the salt water hadn't helped—and the rips would be uncontrollable.

What *was* she saying? What *did* she want from her auntie? Now that Di wasn't taking her to America, shouldn't she get as much as she could from her? No one else would buy her an *ao dai*. So why was she turning it down?

She thought suddenly of the monk's talk, given the Sunday before Di's arrival. The monk had talked of possessions as cows that weighed a person down. And now—she'd never thought it could be true—she felt the burden the *ao dai* would become.

"Are you still holding out for a trip to America?" Di asked, smiling.

"Oh, no." Binh shook her head. She had, really had, given up on that. What *did* she want?

The answer came to her slowly, as though evolving out of the mist. When she spoke, her words also evolved slowly: "I think . . . I'd rather you gave the three hundred thousand *dong* to my family." Spending the money on a pretty outfit would be cruel.

"Give them money? Wouldn't that be rude?"

"Not rude. Not at all," Binh said.

Di sighed. "I just don't understand Vietnamese culture." As though exhausted, she sat down on a low shelf, propping her chin in her hands. "Are you saying," she asked, "that I shouldn't buy anyone in your family anything? That instead they would rather have the money?"

Binh nodded.

"I've been a little blind, Binh. I'm sorry." Di stood up. "I sensed a big need. I thought I could fill it with things like this." She touched a bowl inlaid with bits of iridescent shell. "Or this." She laid an open palm on a stone elephant. "I've been very thoughtless."

A small basket of greeting cards lay on the counter. Di fingered through the pile and chose one picturing two birds. The birds were made of pale straw. "Let's see if I can do better," she said, paying the disappointed shopkeeper.

Chapter Nineteen

A thatched hut served as a bus station. Sitting down on the bench, Di said, "I want to write a little message in this card. But I can't write Vietnamese. Would you?" She held out a pen and the card with the straw birds.

As Di dictated, Binh wrote, slowly and carefully, while her auntie watched. Did she notice how poor Binh's handwriting looked, how much time it took her to write the simple words? Would Di guess her secret?

When the bus came, Di led the way on, choosing two seats in the front. Once they were settled, Binh looked out the window at the pretty town. Even the trunks of the palms were wound with strands of lights.

Di leaned her head back and sighed. "It's been a good day."

The bus rolled out of town and into blackness. Binh dozed, resting against Di's shoulder.

Finally, the engine stopped and Binh looked out to see the restaurant where they'd eaten in the morning. The same street children were already milling around the door of the bus.

"Can we stay inside this time?" Binh asked. She didn't want to see the children again.

"I'm thirsty, Binh. And we both need to stretch our legs," said Di, getting up from her seat.

At the door, the children pressed toward Di. "Madame! Madame!"

"Go away." Binh shooed them.

The children retreated a few steps, then followed Di as she walked to the restaurant.

Di ordered two sodas.

The children hovered nearby, greedy for the sight of an American with money.

"Those boys and girls are here all day and night,"

Di said. "Once their vacation is over, at least they'll be back in school."

They don't go to school, Binh almost said. Instead, she knocked against her drink and spilled it.

Di reached across with a napkin, while Binh just stared at the soda bubbles bursting on the surface of the table. Di assumed the children were on vacation. Did she think that Binh herself was on break and would soon return to school?

The bus driver honked and the passengers stood to leave.

Di handed out money as she passed through the children. "When do *you* go back to school?" she said, relaxing into her seat.

"Never," Binh blurted out.

"What do you mean *never*?" Di's thick American eyebrows met over her nose.

Binh clutched the arm of the seat. The word *never* still vibrated in the air. Why hadn't she thought of a quick lie?

She felt as though she'd fallen into a river current

that carried her against her will. "Those children don't go to school." She waved toward the faces on the other side of the glass, already growing smaller as the bus backed up. "And neither do I."

Just then, the driver turned off the lights inside the bus. Di's voice cut through the sudden darkness. "What do you do instead?"

"I sell fruit and soda. That cart in the backyard . . ."

Di was nodding. "Now I understand. I thought school was out. Yet I saw children in school uniforms. I thought you . . . Why don't you go?" When she turned, Binh smelled the Italian food on her breath.

She waited until the bus turned onto the highway before saying, "Ba can't pay the six hundred thousand *dong* a year for my schooling."

"Six hundred thousand *dong?* I thought school was free in Communist countries."

"School *is* free. But not uniforms or books. Without those, I can't go."

"Six hundred thousand *dong*—that's—mmm . . ."

Di held up her fingers as though counting. "That's only about forty dollars a year. That's not much."

Binh sat up straight. "But Ba doesn't have six hundred thousand extra *dong*."

"I'm sorry, Binh. In America, forty dollars isn't a lot of money. What about Hai? Has he gone to school?"

"Oh, no. Ba Ngoai taught us to read and write a little. I can read all the subtitles in the movies."

"Oh, my." Di laughed, then asked, "What about your cousins?"

"They do what I do. They help with the vegetable garden. Or sell things."

"Well, *you* have to get an education. I'll see to that."

Binh put her hand on Di's forearm and left it there. She recalled the way the ship captain had handed Fourth Uncle the shining red apple. Before biting in, he'd held the apple to the sky. Just so, Binh examined the apple that Di had just handed her, imagining its sweetness.

After a while, Di said sleepily, "I knew I chose the word *Wonder* for a reason."

Binh giggled. Maybe the blue stone hadn't been such a silly gift after all.

"Would Hai like to go to school?" Di asked.

"Anh Hai already has a real job. He has to work."

Binh thought of Cuc unpacking coconut ashtrays in her mother's shop.

Going to school without Cuc, Binh thought, would be like getting on a bus and driving away, leaving Cuc in the darkness.

Binh let several miles go by before she increased the pressure on Di's arm. "Di Hai," she said, willing her voice to rise above the sound of the engine, "could Cuc go to school too?"

"Cuc? What does she do now instead?"

"She helps Third Aunt at the tourist shop."

"Well, if your brother can't go . . ."

Binh held her breath while the bus hurtled through the night.

"Cuc should go."

Binh let her breath out in a long sigh. "Thank you, Di." The imaginary apple was very sweet indeed.

Chapter Twenty

*W*hen the bus pulled into the village, Binh looked out the window to see her family waiting in a line, just as they'd stood in the morning. Once again, Ba and Anh Hai wore their good white shirts, and even though it was very late, Ba Ngoai had come along.

Anh Hai carried a sign that said, *Mung Di Hai va Em tro ve!* Welcome Home, Auntie and Sister!

Her family expected the ocean to be her big news, Binh thought. Goose bumps rose along her arms. Soon they'd learn how much her life was about to change.

Di descended first, and Ba Ngoai drew her daughter to her with a sigh.

Binh stepped down, and everyone pressed close, as though making sure she'd really come home. Even Anh Hai put a hand on her shoulder.

Cuc kicked at the ground. "I bet you had fun."

Binh shrugged. "It was okay." On purpose, she'd left Cuc behind. But now she would make up for it. "Will you come home with us?" Binh held out her hand. "I have something for you."

The white dogs ambled to greet them, and the house smelled of familiar, sweet incense. Bowls of rice and vegetables with bean curd were laid out, ready to eat. Someone had fixed Binh's favorite dish of sliced melon with mint.

Binh smiled at the photographs of the ancestors, wondering if they too were welcoming her home. There, among the offerings of flowers and fruit, lay Di's rocks: *Love, Imagination,* and *Wonder.*

Binh's whole body settled.

"How was the trip?" Anh Hai asked.

"It was exciting. But"—Binh looked around at everyone—"it's also nice to be home."

"Tell us everything," said Ba.

While Di Hai showed the photos on the screen of her camera, Binh told about the ride through the unfamiliar landscape, her first sight of the ocean, the swimming, the foreigners in the tourist town, the odd tastes of the Italian food.

She didn't mention the conversation in the tourist shop.

When the meal had been eaten and the bowls, spoons, and chopsticks placed in the large woven basket, Di took the card from her purse. She looked around as though she didn't know to whom to hand it. Finally, she settled on Ba Ngoai.

Ba Ngoai unsealed the envelope. She held up the card with the straw birds for everyone to admire. When she opened it, a variety of bills fell into her lap.

Binh even saw American money, the green faces of the men looking up at her.

Cuc gasped.

"Dear family," Di said, "from time to time I will be able to spare a little something for you."

Ba passed his hot cup of tea from hand to hand.

Ma glanced up.

Anh Hai studied his fingernails, black with motor-cycle grease.

Ba Ngoai slid closer to Di Thao.

Each of them, Binh saw, was trying to hide a smile.

Di touched Binh's hand. "Now," she whispered.

Binh smiled at the gecko on the ceiling, then spread a hand on each knee. She paused until she had everyone's attention. When they looked to her to speak, she took a big breath and announced: "Di Hai is going to send me to school."

Steam rose from the cups of tea, and beyond, the river danced in the darkness.

Di Thao looked at Ma until Ma nodded slightly.

"I don't have enough money to bring anyone to America," Di said, then paused, letting the words sink in. "But I want to pay for Binh and Cuc to go to school. They need an education."

"Oh! Me too?" Cuc asked, her eyes brightening.

When Di nodded, Cuc climbed over Anh Hai's lap, knocking over a cup of tea, to fling her arms around Di's neck.

Anh Hai winked at Binh, and Binh just smiled.

Chapter Twenty-one

When Binh entered the school surrounded by high walls, she was wearing Cuc's dress with the red flowers. Ba Ngoai had taken up the hem and washed out the smudge of oil from Cuc's bicycle.

As Binh, Cuc, and Di passed through the gate, two roosters strutted across the courtyard. Binh heard the sound of children reciting in one classroom and in another, the voice of a woman reading numbers. She paused.

"Aren't you coming, Binh?" Cuc asked, turning back to her.

Binh drew a circle in the dust with her toe, remembering the many children who'd bought fruit cups and sodas at the cart. She pulled her *non la* low over her eyes. "Do I really belong here?" she whispered to Di.

"As much as anyone," Di said, lifting Binh's hat and looking into her face.

Cuc took her own hat off. "In America," she said, "everyone goes to school."

Di took Binh and Cuc by the hand. Together they marched across the courtyard, sending the roosters scurrying ahead.

Binh saw a woman—was it the one who'd smiled at her the other day?—come out of a classroom.

Binh lifted her hand to wave, and the woman waved back.

Di stopped at a red door with a sign that said *Office*. Letting go of Binh's hand, she turned the knob and went inside.

Mr. Luong, who was also the village mayor, stood to greet them in his black suit and white shirt. A portrait of Ho Chi Minh—with a long, narrow beard—and a yellow hammer and sickle on a red flag hung behind Mr. Luong's desk.

The wall was dirtied at the base where the mop had bumped against it.

"Sit down," said Mr. Luong, pulling up three chairs. The chairs scraped on the tan floor tiles.

Binh noticed that some tiles were perfect squares, others chipped at the edges. She sat down and pulled the skirt of her dress straight. The red flowers bloomed over her knees. She held her *non la* like a soft shield across her chest.

"My name is Sharon Hughes," Di began. "I mean it is Thao . . . uh . . . Hughes. These are my nieces, Binh and Cuc. They will be coming to school here."

"Very good. It is always good to have new students. Welcome, girls."

Binh looked into Mr. Luong's brown eyes.

"They have never been to school," Di said.

Binh blinked at Di's words, as though a bright light had been turned on.

"In that case, they will need to take an examination," Mr. Luong said. "We need to know how much they know."

Mr. Luong didn't seem shocked, Binh noticed. He acted as though entering school so late was normal.

"Does that mean they might be put in with younger children?" Di asked.

"It's a possibility."

Cuc put her hand to her mouth and giggled.

"But only temporarily," Mr. Luong said hastily. "These look like smart girls who will catch up quickly."

Binh hardly cared if she was put in a younger class. She wouldn't sell on the street anymore. She'd become one of those in the blue and white uniforms. She'd learn about the world and hear all the stories she wanted.

At home, Binh slipped her new school uniforms, wrapped in cellophane, underneath the ancestral altar. She lined her new books along the wall and placed a pink dragon on either end.

Di held up the tourist guidebook. "We can get a head start on your education, Binh. This book includes a chapter on the history of Vietnam. I'll translate it for you."

They sat side by side while very slowly, omitting words she didn't know, Di Hai translated the English words into Vietnamese.

Every now and then, she stopped to quiz Binh. "What year did the war with France start? . . . How did China influence Vietnamese culture? . . . Why did the Americans withdraw from the war in 1973?"

They leafed through the guidebook, looking at pictures of a tall waterfall, beaches with jagged rocks rising out of the water, and the wide, green Mekong River.

"It's too bad you've only seen a little bit of Vietnam," Binh said, inching closer to her auntie. Di would go back to America and might never visit these beautiful places.

Di sighed, then smiled. "I guess I'll have to come back, won't I?"

"Oh, yes!" said Binh, taking Di's hand. "Oh, yes!" She flipped to the picture of the waterfall. "When you return, can we go here?" She put her finger on the lacy cascade.

"Of course, Binh. We'll go together."

Binh squeezed Di's hand, and Di squeezed back.

Just as the sun balanced on the horizon, its orange rays passing through the open doorway, Di took the guidebook from Binh. She opened to a new page and said, "And now, let's get back to our studies. It says here that Vietnam is a country moving forward. . . ."

While the sunshine silently entered the room, Binh found herself sitting very close to Di Hai, listening to the story of her country. The color ripened, and Binh watched the transformation of her home: the plain walls, the borrowed motorcycle in the corner, and Ma's stack of *non la*s all aglow. Her world, the center of the world, was being painted with a rich golden light.

Author's Note

In 1975, Operation Babylift flew more than four thousand Vietnamese children out of their country to new homes in America, Canada, Europe, and Australia. Supposedly these children were orphans, but many were not. Some parents hoped that their child would have a chance at a better life in the United States. Many mothers sent children who had American GI fathers. These children were considered *bui doi*, in danger of being killed by the new Communist regime. The Communists had fought against the Americans and regarded these children as enemies. *Bui doi* children who survived were often shunned and mistreated by Vietnamese society.

Glossary and Pronunciation Guide

Anh Hai — oldest brother

ao dai — traditional Vietnamese dress consisting of trousers with a long tunic on top

areca palm — a species of palm tree found in much of Asia; chewing the nut or leaves can stain the teeth and gums red.

Ba — father

Ba Ngoai — maternal grandmother (pronounced "BAH ngoy")

Binh — (pronounced "bin")

bui doi—literally means "less than dust"; refers to a person of mixed blood

cai coc—hut

Chau—grandchild, a term of endearment

Chi—sister. A younger sister must address her older sister as Chi, as in Chi Thao.

Chi Hai—eldest sister

con—child

con cung—spoiled little child, a term of endearment

Cuc—(pronounced "kook")

Di—aunt (pronounced "yee")

Di Hai—eldest aunt

dong—unit of Vietnamese money; approximately sixteen thousand *dong* equal one U.S. dollar. Only bills are used.

ganh hang—a contraption consisting of a bamboo pole carried over the shoulders with a flat, round basket hanging from each end of the pole

Hai—word used to indicate the eldest of a group

Ma—mother

mangosteen—a dark purple fruit, white on the inside

Mung Di Hai va Em tro ve!—Welcome Home, Auntie and Sister!

non la—cone-shaped traditional Vietnamese straw hat

pho bo—traditional Vietnamese beef noodle soup

rambutan—a bright red fruit, white on the inside

tam cuc—a card game

Thao—(pronounced "tao")

Viet-kieu—Vietnamese who live abroad

ACKNOWLEDGMENTS

I would like to give credit to the KPBS documentary *Daughter from Danang* for its sensitive portrayal of a situation very like Binh's. I would also like to acknowledge Brother Phap Khoi of Deer Park Monastery for his monitoring of cultural details; Helen Tonnu for her detailed instructions on the making of the traditional cone-shaped hats; Gretchen Woelfle for her readings of the manuscript in its early form; Janice Yuwiler for her support and collaborative brainstorming; and my editors, Deborah Wayshak and Amy Ehrlich, who guided me, as always, toward the truest form of the story.